PRAISE FOR DIANA PALMER

"Nobody tops Diana Palmer
when it comes to delivering pure,
undiluted romance. I love her stories."
—*New York Times* bestselling author Jayne Ann Krentz

"Diana Palmer is a mesmerizing storyteller who
captures the essence of what a romance should be."
—*Affaire de Coeur*

"Diana Palmer is a unique talent
in the romance industry. Her writing
combines wit, humor, and sensuality;
and, as the song says, nobody does it better!"
—*New York Times* bestselling author Linda Howard

"No one beats this author for sensual anticipation."
—*Rave Reviews*

"A love story that is pure and enjoyable."
—*Romantic Times* on *Lord of the Desert*

"The dialogue is charming, the characters
likable and the sex sizzling..."
—*Publishers Weekly* on *Once in Paris*

Diana Palmer has published over seventy category romances, as well as historical romances and longer contemporary works. With over 40 million copies of her books in print, Diana Palmer is one of North America's most beloved authors. Her accolades include two *Romantic Times Magazine* Reviewer's Choice Awards, a Maggie Award, five national Waldenbooks bestseller awards and two national B. Dalton bestseller awards. Diana resides in the north mountains of her home state of Georgia with her husband, James, and their son, Blayne Edward.

DIANA PALMER

Bound by a Promise

Silhouette Books

Published by Silhouette Books
America's Publisher of Contemporary Romance

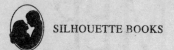 SILHOUETTE BOOKS

ISBN 0-373-63188-X

BOUND BY A PROMISE

First published in North America as a MacFadden Romance by Kim Publishing Corporation.

Visit Silhouette at www.eHarlequin.com

Printed in U.S.A.

One

He was standing alone by the shore, a big, solitary figure against the thin mist that blanketed the silvery water in the early morning. Kathryn had seen him there before a number of times since she and Maude had moved into the lake house for the summer. But keeping up with the famous author's blazing deadlines had only allowed for a few brief outings on the lake for Kate, one of which the man standing there had shattered with his arrogance.

Kathryn Summers was curious about Garet Cambridge, even while she resented everything he stood for. His aircraft corporation was one of the biggest in the country, and his genius for designing new planes had earned him an international reputation. But all it meant to Kathryn was that he could buy people.

She knew too much about prices already, having just been thrown over by the man she loved when he found out that her social pedigree didn't meet his family's exacting standards. The daughter of a small Texas cattle rancher whose parents were divorced was hardly a likely candidate for the social register. In fact, it was only this job, working for the notorious Maude Niccole, that made it possible for her to keep her father's ranch from being put on the auction block. His health was steadily failing, and so were the ranch's profits.

She glared at Cambridge unconsciously from her perch on a log beside the spreading waters of Lake Lanier. She'd come here for the peace and quiet, and she wished he'd decided to spend his summer in Europe or Miami instead of here. Perhaps he thought the reporters who trailed him might not think of looking for him on a North Georgia lake. And apparently they hadn't, because he was alone; a ghostly figure in brown slacks and a cream open-necked sports shirt, his dark hair lifting in the breeze.

As if he felt the intensity of emotion in the glare of her pale brown eyes, he turned suddenly and saw her sitting there, with her silver blonde hair flowing down like silk around her thin shoulders.

He moved forward with his hands in his pockets until he was standing over her, towering over her, and his leaf green eyes glittered down at her out of a face as dark as an Indian's.

"You're trespassing," he said gruffly, not even bothering with polite conversation.

She cocked her head up at him. "Excuse me, I wasn't aware that you owned the shoreline as well as the lake," she said bitterly, referring to an earlier incident between them, when he'd practically ordered her off the lake.

One dark eyebrow went up at the sarcasm. "I own 50 acres of shoreline," he said quietly. "What you're sitting on is part of it. I came here for privacy, not to be hounded by curiosity seekers."

She'd have given anything at that moment to have had wealth enough, power enough, to tell him where to go. But she had nothing, and he could force her to go easily enough. She got up from the stump without another word, brushing off her blue denim jeans. With a sigh of resignation, she started back toward Maude's luxurious beach house.

"Who are you?" he growled after her.

"Amelia Earhardt," she replied carelessly. "Do keep your eyes peeled for my plane, I seem to have misplaced it," she added, and kept right on walking.

Behind her, she imagined she heard the deep sound of a man's laughter.

Maude was waiting for her in the sprawling living room, her bags packed, her thin face nervous.

"Thank goodness, you're back!" the novelist sighed. "I thought you'd never come home! Kate, I've just gotten a telegram. My father's in the hospital, and I've got to fly to Paris immediately."

"I'm sorry," Kate said with genuine concern.

"So am I," Maude said sadly. "I'm very fond of the old scalawag, even if he did disown me when I announced that I'd decided to become a romance writer. Honey, will you be okay here until I get back? I don't have any idea how long it's going to take."

Kate nodded and smiled, hating that drawn, hurt look on her employer's face, the sadness in Maude's pale blue eyes framed by salt and pepper curly hair. "I'll finish typing the manuscript while you're gone."

Maude nodded, looking around to see if she'd forgotten anything. "Don't overlook that page of changes I wrote last night—I think it's in the top desk drawer. And, for goodness sake, keep your door locked at night!"

"I will. Don't worry about me."

"I can't help it," Maude said with a quick smile. "You're so reckless lately, Kate. Is it the job? Do you want out?''

"No, it's not that," came the quick reply. "I...oh, I don't know, maybe it's the weather. It's so hot.''

"The weather, or memories?" the older woman probed. "Jesse Drewe was a triple-A heel, my love, you deserve better.''

Kate shifted from one foot to the other restlessly. "I'd have liked to be turned down for myself," she said softly, "not for my lack of money and social standing. It hurt.''

"I know, but we don't always love to order," Maude said, "and more's the pity. You'll get over it. I know you don't think so now, but you will.''

"Of course," Kate said, even though she didn't believe it. "Have a safe trip, and let me know you got there all right.''

"I'll send you a cable, I promise," Maude replied. "Where were you, anyway?'' she asked idly as she picked up one suitcase, leaving the other for Kate to bring as she went out the door and headed for the rented car.

"On the beach," she replied. "At least I was until Mr. Cambridge Aircraft Corporation ordered me off his lake."

"Garet again?" Maude sighed. "Oh, Kate, why can't you be kind to that man? You've already had one run-in with him over the way you were speeding in the boat...."

"He doesn't own the lake," Kate said stubbornly, remembering too well the cold voice telling her if she didn't stop 'driving over the lake like a maniac' he'd have the lake patrol after her. She'd told him where to go, recognizing him immediately from photos she'd seen in news magazines, and zoomed off in Maude's little light cruiser. Since that day, she'd seen him often walking alone on the beach, but he'd never spoken to her again, and she'd never allowed him close enough to make it possible.

"He owns enough of the lake," Maude replied. She took Kate by the shoulders, smiling at her sullen look. "Don't match wits with him. He can hurt you. Don't try to make him pay for Jesse's behavior. Jesse was only a boy. Garet..." she paused, searching for the words, "Garet's a law unto himself. He makes up his own rules as he goes along. Be careful you don't break any of them. He makes an utterly ruthless enemy."

"How do you know?" Kate asked.

"I was a reporter before I got smart and started writing books," Maude explained. "I did a story about Garet and misquoted one of his top advisers. He had me fired, and every time I tried to apply for another position, I seemed to be wrong for the job. Finally, in desperation, I sent Garet a lengthy, tearful apology, and the next thing I knew, editors were calling me in for interviews.'' She smiled. ''It was a rough way to learn the necessity for accuracy. I never forgot the lesson.''

Kate felt chills run up and down her spine despite the heat. ''He sounds like a bulldozer.''

''He is,'' Maude agreed. ''It takes a ruthless man to build an empire, and to hold it.''

''I pity his wife.''

''He doesn't have one.''

''I'm not surprised!''

''He has women instead,'' Maude grinned. ''His own personal harem, and they drip jewels and mink.''

''Money can buy everything, it seems,'' Kate grumbled, feeling the hurt all over again.

''Not everything, baby. Not love.'' Maude got into the rented car and closed the door. ''I don't know when I'll get to come home. When you finish the manuscript, mail it to Benny and start working on the next one I've drafted on tape. Okay?''

''Okay.'' Kate squeezed the thin hand through the open window. ''Thank you,'' she added.

''For what?''

''For hiring me. For caring about me. For putting up with me,'' Kate said, her eyes like burnished gold in her oval face.

Maude smiled. ''Who puts up with whom?'' she corrected. ''Little one, I'm quite fond of you. If I'd had the good sense to marry in my youth, I'd have a daughter your age. Lonely people seem to find each other.''

''I'm not lonely,'' Kate told her, with a smile. ''Not now.''

''Yes, you are,'' the older woman replied kindly, searching the pale brown eyes. ''Lonely and hurting. But we have to weather the storms before we can enjoy the sunshine. Don't dwell on the past, and the sun will come out a lot faster.''

''Take care,'' Kate said softly.

Maude only laughed. ''I'm indestructible, didn't you know?'' she teased.

''I hope it goes well.''

''He's seventy-eight,'' Maude reminded her. ''He's lived a long life, and a full one. I won't pretend that I can give him up without tears. But I'll cross that bridge when I have to. Meanwhile, I've got to get there. Remember what I said, and don't speed in the boat,'' she added, emphasizing each word.

''Killjoy,'' Kate grinned. ''Okay, I'll hunt bears.''

Maude lifted her eyes heavenward. ''They say that God looks after fools and children. I do hope it's true. Bye, honey.''

She was off in a cloud of dust, and

Kate watched until the car was a speck in the distance.

The big log beach house was empty without Maude's sparkling personality. Kate mooned around drinking coffee and staring out at the tree-edged lake as it shimmered in the sunlight like silver, rippling cloth.

Maude was right, she did have to let go of the past. But how could she, when every time she closed her eyes she saw Jesse's long, smiling face, the blue eyes that laughed and loved her.

She'd met Jesse in Austin, where she and her father had gone to a cattle sale, and they were fast friends before the day was over. Jesse had a sophistication she'd never been exposed to in the rural area where she lived, a charm that knocked her legs out from under her. By the time he took her back to her hotel, her heart was in bars. And judging by the way he kissed her goodnight, it seemed as if the feeling might be mutual.

The sale had lasted three days, and Kate the rancher's daughter and Jesse the meatpacker's son were inseparable. In between meals, they acted like tourists, seeing every interesting spot in the city and outside it, learning how much they had in common, clinging to each other with a desperation that was like an omen of things to come.

On the third day, he asked her to marry him, and she said yes. She was that sure, even after such a short space of time. What she hadn't counted on was the new social set it would throw her into.

Jesse wanted to take her home with him, to introduce her to his family. Kate was reluctant, but she saw the inevitability of it. And her father let her go readily enough, even though the trip to Chicago would wipe out her savings. He had wished her happiness with twinkling brown eyes.

They'd no sooner arrived at Jesse's family's estate outside Chicago when Kate began to open her eyes to reality. The house was old, and elegant, and dripping in crystal chandeliers, and Victorian wing chairs which weren't reproductions. As if the trappings weren't enough to bring the situation home to her, Jesse's mother came down the stairs in an original Oleg Cassini gown, perfectly coiffed, and reeking of expensive perfume. To say she wasn't impressed with Kate was an understatement. She took the young girl's hand as if she were picking up a dead mouse, dropping it as quickly as possible and calling her husband downstairs with a voice that positively quavered with horror.

Kate was uncomfortable to the point of tears, even with Jesse's half-hearted reassurances. But at the dinner table when his father pinned her down about the actual size of her father's cattle ranch and she told them 100 acres, Jesse looked as if he might faint. That was when she understood the mistaken impression he'd had of the ranch. He'd thought she was one of "his kind" of people, and had suddenly found to his astonishment that she was almost penniless.

The next day, Jesse's mother called Kate into the study, and, with a frozen smile, explained that Jesse had been called away on urgent business. She hoped Kate hadn't taken Jesse seriously, the boy was so young, and a little flighty, and so easily taken in by a pretty face. Kate would get over it, and, anyway, hadn't she enjoyed seeing how the other half lived and having her breakfast served in bed?

Wounded, hurting, dying inside, Kate managed to say the right thing, pack her bag, and with her savings, af-

ford a bus ticket home to Texas. The
money she'd had to spend getting
home would have gone to help pay off
the heavy mortgage on her father's
ranch. Only Maude's advertisement in
the Austin paper had saved them from
foreclosure. That was several months
ago, but the wounds were still open
and every thought of the Drewe family,
or great wealth, rubbed more salt in
them.

Rich people could get away with
murder. They owned the world and all
the little people in it, and they could
do as they liked with their victims.
Kate only wished she had that kind of
power; enough to make the Drewes
squirm as they'd made her squirm,
enough to teach them an unforgettable
lesson in humiliation.

It ached, the memory ached inside
her, and she couldn't stand the confines
of the cabin another instant. Despite
Maude's warning, she went straight to

the small cabin cruiser and cranked it. Gently, she eased it away from the pier and out of the cove, speeding up as she hit the wide open waters of the lake. There were a few other boats out, but not many this early in the morning. Kate had most of the wide blue expanse to herself, and she opened up the throttle, feeling the boat smash through the waves, feeling the spray in her face, vibrantly biting, taking away the pain, easing the hurt. She drew in a deep breath of the cool, sweet air with its faint fragrance of honeysuckle. A smile touched her flushed face, the wildness of speed made her eyes sparkle darkly behind her closed eyelids. What bliss, to let the spray and the wind cut away the memories!

She opened her eyes again and felt her heart stop. She grabbed feverishly for the throttle as she saw the dark spot in her path, growing with incredible speed in size, into a recognizable shape.

"Mr. Cambridge, look out!" she screamed, her eyes widening with horror as they gaped at the dark wet head and wide bronzed shoulders looming just ahead.

He half turned in the water, his eyes spotting her at the wheel. Just before the bow of the cabin cruiser struck, she saw him dive under the surface.

She fought to get the boat under control, her panic sending it around in circles before she finally got it stopped and let it drift aimlessly while she hung over the side with her heart machine-gunning in her chest, searching the choppy waters in quiet desperation. Had she killed him?!

Two

It was the longest ten seconds of her life until Garet Cambridge's dark head appeared above the surface of the water, with blood pouring from a deep gash at the back of his head. He was near the pier that led to his massive cabin and, as she watched, stricken, he felt for the floating pontoons that held the pier up and heaved himself unsteadily onto the weathered gray boards, breathing heavily.

She breathed a sigh of relief. Thank God he was all right! She started the boat and circled it around going slowly now, not rushing, trembling with guilt and fear and relief. She glanced back to see Cambridge sitting up on the pier, sucking in deep breaths.

Almost a tragedy, but not quite. Almost a tragedy, because of her recklessness, because she wanted to use speed to relieve her pain and, in doing so, had almost cost a man his life. The fact that she didn't like Cambridge was no reason to run him down; but she hadn't done it on purpose, she hadn't! What would he do, she wondered. Would he press charges? Would he have her arrested? Did she only imagine that she saw recognition in those dark green eyes just before she plowed over him?

She floated the cruiser and silently

watched Cambridge as he raised his
husky frame and staggered down the
pier to his cabin. She was crying so
hard she could hardly think straight,
and the words that she wanted to call
out to him stuck fast in her throat. Her
first impulse was to dock her boat in
Cambridge's pier and follow him up to
his cabin. But then as she floated
nearer, she saw several people meeting
Cambridge at the door. Their sounds of
surprise and concern drifted across the
lake as they crowded around him and
ushered him within. Then the door
closed and she could only assume that
in the excitement, no one had noticed
her boat, just a short distance from the
dock.

The thought of facing the injured
Cambridge was bad enough, but she
simply wasn't able to summon the
courage it would take to face both him
and his crowd of friends. At least she
was sure now that he would be well

taken care of. She floated the cruiser beside the pier and into the boat house, locking it up. Then she went into the cabin and threw herself down on the couch. She held her face in her hands and allowed her tears to run freely. If only Maude were here, she thought....

When the tears finally passed, she sat up and dried her eyes and tried to decide what to do. Should she call Cambridge and ask how he was and try to explain, to apologize? Should she report the accident to the lake patrol? Should she call a doctor? What if he'd been hurt worse than she thought? It was a hard knock, and a lot of blood...what if he died? She felt panic like a sick lump lodge deep in her throat. If he died, she'd be guilty of murder!

But if she gave herself in, and he wasn't badly hurt at all? What if he hadn't known it was she who hurt him, wouldn't he prosecute her without hesitation, knowing how reckless she'd already been with the boat? And if she was in jail, there'd be no way to help her father out of debt!

Her mind flashed with activity. No one witnessed the accident. She wasn't known on the lake, only Cambridge had even seen her enough to recognize her. Of course, he'd have recognized the boat, possibly, even if he hadn't identified Kate. But the boat was nothing special, and he didn't know Kate's name, after all.

She licked her lips nervously. Still, what if he was badly hurt?

She lifted the phone and waited for the dial tone. By a stroke of luck she didn't expect, Cambridge's number was listed. She dialed the number. She had to know, even it if meant going to prison. She had to make sure he was going to be all right.

A soft, feminine voice answered the phone. "Hello?"

Kate swallowed, and tried to disguise her voice, to deepen it. "Is Mr. Cambridge in?" she asked in what she hoped was a calm, businesslike tone.

"No, he's been taken to the hospital," came the easy reply. "An accident. We think he must have fallen and hit his head on something. He was bleeding pretty badly, but he was cursing pretty badly, too, so Bob and I think he'll be okay. Is this Pattie?"

With closed eyes and a shuddering sigh, Kate hung up. He was alive. He was all right. She hadn't killed him, thank God. But there in the back of her mind, she remembered what Maude had said about the industrial magnate—that he made a ruthless enemy, and he always got even. Would he, somehow, make her pay for what she'd done? Did he know that it was her fault, would he hunt for her?

She didn't go outside again. There were plenty of groceries in the pantry and she could last indefinitely if she had to. She was terrified that if she went on the beach, he might be there, he might recognize her. Even hidden like this, she dreaded the day when a knock on the door would come, or the phone would ring, and she'd be forced to pay for her carelessness. She felt like a condemned criminal. But her own guilt was punishing her more than any court could.

When the phone finally did ring, several days later, she jumped like a thief. She let it ring four times before she summoned enough nerve to lift the receiver.

"H...hello?" she whispered.

"Miss Summers? Miss Kathryn Summers?" a woman's voice queried.

"Yes," she managed, her eyes closing with something akin to relief. It was all over now.

"I have a telegram for you from Miss Maude Niccole in Paris," the woman said cheerfully, and Kate's heart stopped, then started beating again. "Father doing well. Stop. Must stay for few weeks. Stop. Close cabin and go home for present. Stop. Will explain in letter. Stop. Love, Maude."

Kate thanked the operator and hung up, feeling lost and alone and afraid. Did she dare go home and expose her father to the possible consequences of her actions? He had a bad heart, and any shock could cost him his life.

What if Garet Cambridge came looking for her and had her prosecuted, could her father bear the shock when he learned what his daughter had done? He'd raised her to care about other people, to be responsible for herself. Was the way she was acting responsible? She sighed. There was only one thing left to do. The thing she should have had the courage to do in the first place. She was going to have to go to Cambridge and tell him the whole story and throw herself on his mercy—if there was any in him. Which she doubted.

Like a lamb heading for the gate to the slaughterhouse, she braved the outside world and strode reluctantly along the beach in her white shorts and top, her eyes downcast as she counted rocks along the shoreline and dreaded the inevitable.

She was so lost in thought that she was almost on top of the big, dark figure before she stopped with a gasp, almost colliding with him in the process.

He turned and she found herself looking straight into Garet Cambridge's dark green eyes, and her heart froze in her chest.

"Excuse me," she managed in a husky whisper, her voice unnaturally tight as she strained for the right words. "I..."

"My fault," he replied with deadly calm. He raised a smoking cigarette to his chiseled mouth and took a long draw. "I can't see you."

She gaped at him incredulously, at the unseeing green eyes, the unblinking gaze of the blind as he stared straight ahead.

"Your...eyes?" she managed. The world was falling in on her.

"An accident," he replied. "They tell me I fell. I'll be damned if I remember anything about it except a blinding pain. Is it dark yet?"

She shook her head dazedly and then, realizing that he couldn't see the gesture, she said, "No, not yet."

He sighed wearily. His dark face was drawn, heavily lined, as if he'd known a great deal of pain in recent days. Kate choked back a sob, the realization of just exactly how much damage she'd done hitting her all at once. She'd blinded him!

"I like this time of day," he said conversationally. "The peace of it. It's a damned far cry from horns and traffic and gaudy music."

She studied him quietly. "Do you...do you come from a place like this?" she asked softly, hoping he wouldn't recognize her voice. Although, she thought, he hadn't really heard it enough to recognize it.

A mocking smile curled his lips. "In a sense, I live in the city. You?"

"I grew up on a ranch," she murmured.

"A cowgirl?" he asked.

She laughed. "More of a milkmaid," she admitted, surprised at this very human side of the man she'd hated by reputation, by previous contact.

"Well, milkmaid, what are you doing on the lake?"

Paying for every sin I ever committed, she thought shakily. "I'm having a holiday with a friend," she said.

"Male or female?" he asked with a half smile.

"Female, of course," she told him indignantly.

The smile widened. "There's no 'of course' about it these days," he replied. "Has your life been that sheltered?"

"In a way," she nodded. "Rural people...I suppose we aren't very worldly."

"How rural are you?"

"Texas," she grinned involuntarily.

"What part?"

"Near Austin," she said quickly, without thinking, and could have bitten her tongue for it.

"Your family are in cattle, I take it?" he asked carelessly.

"My father," she corrected, "has five hundred cows, most of which he's already had to sell off because of the drought. I'm not well-to-do," she added flatly. "When I was little, it was all Dad could do to keep me in shoes and sweaters."

"Touchy, aren't you?" he asked pleasantly.

"Yes," she admitted, wrapping her arms around her as if she felt a sudden chill. "What do you do for a living?" she asked with practised carelessness.

His dark face clouded, his unseeing eyes narrowed. He took a long draw from his cigarette. "I...was a pilot," he said finally.

She gaped at him. He was lying to her, deliberately it seemed, too. Why?

"What kind of planes did you fly?" she probed gently.

He smiled. "Untested ones."

"You were a test pilot?" she asked, and it suddenly came to her that he tested the very planes he designed; a dangerous undertaking for a man with his wealth, and unnecessary.

"That's it." He drew a deep breath. "Needless to say, I won't be doing it any longer. I'm in the market for a new profession.''

''Is there...can you do something besides fly?'' she asked, studying the tall, brooding figure beside her as she dropped down onto a fallen tree and watched him.

''I thought I might do a book on airplanes,'' he replied. He laughed softly. ''By God, I've had enough experience with them to tell a few tales.''

''From test pilot to writer?'' she teased softly. ''Can you write?''

He turned toward the sound of her voice and looked down his nose in her general direction. ''I can do damned near anything that pleases me, Miss,'' he replied coolly. ''You're an impertinent brat, aren't you?''

''How do you know I'm a brat?'' she returned.

''Your voice. You sound as if you're barely out of your teens.''

''Well, I am,'' she retorted, shaking

back her pale hair. "I'm twenty-two, almost twenty-three."

He lifted his cigarette to his lips. "Twenty-two," he murmured softly. "What a magic age that was. All the world to pick and choose from, and no barriers at all in the way."

"It isn't exactly like that," she replied.

"Wait until you reach my age, little one, and tell me again."

She studied the dark, leonine head with its sprinkling of gray hairs that turned silver in the fading sunset light. "I didn't realize you were such a relic," she murmured with careful irony. "Goodness, I'd never have guessed you were actually in your fifties."

Both dark eyebrows shot up. "What?!"

"Well, you said..."

"I'm forty, damn it!" he growled.

"And I can still run circles around men half my age!"

She didn't doubt it, that muscular physique didn't have a spare ounce of flab on it. He was strong, and it showed in every line.

"On foot, or on a motorbike?" she asked conversationally.

"Damn you," he laughed, a deep, pleasant sound in the stillness, that was only broken by the lap of water at the shore's edge.

"No manners, either, I see," she teased.

His eyes narrowed, glittered at the sound of her voice. "Women have been drowned for less."

"By you?"

"I've never been tempted like this before," he told her.

"Maybe I'd better go before you get violent," she suggested.

"That might not be a bad idea. Is it dark?"

She glanced toward the horizon. "Very nearly," she said, watching the sun go down in flames behind the silvery lake, the silhouette of tall pines.

"It isn't wise for a young woman to wander around here in the dark," he cautioned.

"What about you?" she asked as she turned to go.

His eyebrows went up. "I don't really expect that a would-be attacker would mistake me for a woman," he said bluntly.

Looking at the big, husky body, she seriously doubted it, too, and the idea tickled her so that a soft laugh broke from her lips.

"What are you snickering at?" he demanded.

"The thought of anyone mistaking you for a woman."

He chuckled softly. "I see your point. Go home."

"But, can you find your way back…?"

"Why? Are you afraid I'll trip over my feet and fall in the lake?" he asked.

"It gets very deep very fast they say," she replied.

"I've only been like this for a little over a week," he told her quietly, "but I'm not helpless. I may burn a few holes in my chair, and I run into door facings and step on the dog's tail, but I…what's so damned funny?"

She forced herself to stop giggling. "It's the way you put things," she told him. "I'm not laughing at you, but…oh, the poor dog!"

"Oh, the poor dog, hell! He's a 130-pound gray shepherd, and he's got the disposition of a rattlesnake with a can tied to his tail."

"Anyway," she persisted, watching his face, "you don't have anybody to get you home, and no cane…"

"I have a houseboy named Yama

who'll be out here on his knees with a flashlight and a net, dredging the lake, if I'm not back by dark,'' he replied smoothly. ''Very handy, is Yama. Not at all like some of my faithful few who turned tail and ran when they were told that I couldn't see.''

''They couldn't have been very faithful,'' she observed. ''Do...do you know if you might regain your sight?''

He drew a deep breath and she stiffened, tensed, waiting for the answer. ''There's a chance,'' he replied. ''A very good one, that my sight will return normally, without surgical intervention. But how soon...no one knows. It could be days, or weeks, or months—or never. It was a hard blow, however it happened, and a tremendous shock to the optic nerve.''

She swallowed. ''Can you see at all?''

He smiled wistfully. ''Dark blobs; a few shadows.''

She blinked back tears. She couldn't cry, she didn't dare. "Well, I'd better go home."

"How far is it?" he asked suddenly.

"Just down the beach," she said carefully.

"What's your name?" The question was sharp, quick.

"Kate," she replied. "Kate... Jones," she added untruthfully, to throw him off the track. "Well, good-bye...."

"Kate!"

She turned. "Yes?"

"Come tomorrow."

The request shocked her—if it was a request. He'd made it sound like a royal command. Getting too close to him now could be horribly dangerous. But when she saw the quiet anguish in his face that peeked for an instant out of the impassive mask he wore, she couldn't refuse.

"Here?" she asked in a thin voice.

"At the cabin. About nine in the morning. I'll have Yama set breakfast for two. How about it?" he added gruffly, as if he wasn't used to making requests and hated even the idea of asking for anything.

"Can I have bacon?" she asked.

"Sure."

"How about coffee?"

"Done."

"Maybe a bagel with dark honey and hand-crushed mangoes?" she teased.

"Keep it up and all you'll get is the coffee," he returned.

"Coffee's better than nothing, I suppose. Good night."

There was a pause as she started off down the beach. "Good night...Kate," he said softly, and the words echoed along behind her like some ghostly echo.

She slept for the first night in days, relieved that there was even a chance he might recover, even while she was torn by regret and guilt for having done this to him. He was so different from what she'd expected, and plainly reluctant to tell her the truth about himself; that he owned a gigantic corporation, that he was wealthy enough to satisfy almost any material hunger he possessed. It was almost as if he were playing some kind of game...could it be that he knew who she was? She shook her head. No, he wouldn't have been friendly, he wouldn't have invited her to breakfast, if he'd known she was the reckless woman who cost him his sight and so much pain.

She was still worrying over it the next morning when she went to the front door of his spacious beach house and knocked.

A small, slender Oriental opened the door with a smile and welcomed her.

"Come in, come in," he said with only a trace of an accent. "Mr. Cambridge been pacing floor since seven. He waits for you on porch, please go ahead. Breakfast is on its way.''

She thanked him with a smile and followed the direction he'd pointed out onto a screened in porch with a magnificent view of the lake.

Cambridge was there, his hands locked behind him, wearing white Bermuda shorts and a white knit top that displayed his dark, muscular arms to a distinct advantage. He seemed to be staring out at the lake, but she knew, full well, that he wasn't seeing it.

''Good morning,'' she said hesitantly.

He turned quickly, his blind eyes searching, as if by looking hard enough he might be able to find her.

''Good morning. Won't you sit down?''

She helped herself to the chair across from what was obviously his. ''I like your porch,'' she told him.

"So do I. The screens keep the mos-
quitoes away," he chuckled.

"It's so peaceful here," she murmured, closing her eyes so that she
could hear, even better, the whisper of
wind through the tall pines, the soft
lapping sound the water made against
the shore.

"That's why I like it," he replied.
"Yama, I'm starving to death out
here!" he bellowed toward the kitchen.

"No need to shout, I come as
quickly as possible," Yama fussed,
bringing in a tray laden with food and
a huge pot of coffee. He began to ar-
range it on the table. "Always, you
nag, but if I bring the food when you
say, you always complain eggs not
done enough, bacon not crisp
enough...."

"How would you like a nice, fat
raise, Yama?" Cambridge asked
through narrowed blank eyes.

Yama's lean face brightened. "That would be very nice, sir."

"Good. Maybe when you learn not to complain so much, I'll get around to giving you one."

Yama made a face at him. "One must be saint to put up with you. Instead of pay hike, I should get medal."

Kate couldn't repress a laugh as Yama disappeared. "He's an absolute jewel," she said.

"Amen, but he won't let me take myself seriously, and I suppose that's an asset." He took a long, deep breath. "He's been with me so long, it would be like losing an arm if he left."

"Does he go everywhere with you?"

A slow, easy smile touched his wide mouth. "Not everywhere," he said in a meaningful tone.

"That's not what I meant."

"Do you blush?" he asked suddenly.

"Of course not!" she lied.

He chuckled softly. "Somehow I don't believe you."

"Do you come to the lake a lot?" she asked quickly, sipping the hot, black coffee that Yama had poured.

"Not any more," he replied. He reached for his coffee cup and upset it, blistering his big hand, and let out a string of blue words.

Kate got to her feet automatically with her napkin and wrapped it around the warm hand, gently removing the liquid from his broad, strong fingers. It was a beautifully masculine hand, she thought involuntarily, noticing the dark, crisp hairs that grew on its back, the square, well-manicured nails. It was warm and a little calloused, and holding it made her tingle with a strange, unfamiliar excitement.

"I'm all right," he said gruffly, but he didn't try to pull his hand away.

"Hurt, didn't it?" she asked with a smile.

"Like hell. I told you I knocked things over."

"I would have taken your word for it, you know," she teased, and let go of his hand to mop up the dark stains growing on the pure white tablecloth.

He chuckled softly. "You're good for me, you little brat. No sympathy in you, is there?"

"Do you want me to coo and fuss over you?"

He scowled in her general direction. "What did you say you do for a living?" he asked, ignoring her attempt at humor.

"I'm a secretary, usually," she replied. "Why?"

"Are you tied up for the rest of the summer?" he persisted.

"Well, not for a few weeks," she admitted, confused by his dogged tone.

"Then why don't you move in with me?" he asked bluntly.

Three

She sat gaping at him, her voice gone, her eyes about to pop with the shock.

A slow, knowing smile touched the wide contours of his mouth. "I'm not asking you to share my bed, if that's what produced this deafening silence," he said. "The idea of making love to a woman I can't see doesn't have much appeal right now, Kate."

She blushed, and turned her face

away before she remembered that he couldn't see her. What was he asking? And she didn't dare live under the same roof with him. What if she trapped herself, and she might, by giving away that she'd been the maniac in the boat that struck him. What might he do? She remembered Maude's warning, about how ruthless he could be, and she was afraid of what his power could do, not only to her, but to her father. Yet, how could she turn her back on him now, when just about everybody else in his life seemed to have done just that? And Maude had told her to take a few weeks off and close up the cabin....

"I'd pay you your regular salary, plus," Cambridge said quietly. "Although I won't promise you regular hours, Kate. Sometimes I hurt like hell in the middle of the night, and dictating something for the book might ease the pain."

"You...want me to help you put the book together?" she asked.

"I can't do it alone, and Yama can cook, but he can't type." His lips set. "Is it the thought of working for a blind man that puts you off, Kate?" he asked tightly.

"Why should it?" she asked without thinking.

He seemed to relax a little. "You'd have free time," he promised. "You like the lake, don't you? If your friend wouldn't mind...?"

"Oh, she wouldn't mind, that's not it." She searched for an excuse that wouldn't wound him. "It's just...we don't know each other."

"I'm not proposing marriage," he chuckled. "We don't have to be on intimate terms for you to be my secretary."

"I'm glad of that," she said uneasily, "because I wouldn't know how."

There was a long pause. "I wish I

could see you," he said finally. "But you don't sound very worldly, Kate, if that's anything to go on."

"I never wanted to be. I don't care much for material things."

"What do you care for?" he probed.

"Gardens," she said with a smile. "Cows gathering in a pasture late in the afternoon. Children in clean pajamas right after a bath. Those kinds of things."

He leaned back in his chair. "I've never known any of those," he said matter-of-factly. "I live my life on a roller coaster that never stops. If I'm not on the phone, I'm in conference. If I'm not sleeping, I'm traveling."

"I guess a pilot's life does get pretty hectic," she remarked, as she remembered the half-truth he'd told her and played along with him.

He reached in his pocket for a cigarette and rolled it absently in his strong fingers. "That wasn't exactly the whole truth. I designed planes, and did my own testing most of the time. I...needed the element of danger, milk-maid,'' he sighed. Something painful came and went in his eyes. ''Have you ever felt that way?''

''Yes, I have,'' she admitted, hating the memory of what she'd done to this man, whose eyes were everything to him.

''Why?'' he asked bluntly.

She shifted restlessly in her chair, cupping her slender hands around her coffee cup. ''I was in love with a man who thought I had money. When he found out I didn't, he couldn't get rid of me fast enough.'' Put like that, it sounded so simple, so uncomplicated, and yet it had tormented her for months.

''Not good enough for him, Kate?'' he asked. He put the cigarette to his mouth and fumbled with his lighter until he managed to light it. "What did his family own?"

"A meat processing plant."

He chuckled softly. "Only one? My God, they were low on the social ladder."

"I don't understand."

"I'll teach you about stocks and investments one day, and you will." He drew in a breath of smoke. "Baby, one meat processing plant is like owning one tiny business in a town where another man owns a city block. Does that clarify it a little?"

"A little," she said. "I don't know about being rich. I never was. I don't think I'd like it. I'm a lot more comfortable in jeans and T-shirts than I am in evening gowns."

"Money has advantages and disadvantages," he agreed. "Well, Kate, are you going to move in with me or not?"

"I probably ought to have my head examined..."

"Assuredly, both of us should. Yes or no?"

"Yes."

"Good girl. Finish your breakfast and I'll introduce you to the hairy member of my family."

"Hairier than you?" she asked in mock astonishment, her eyes on the thick pelt of black hair that showed in the neck of his open-throated white shirt.

"I hope you can keep that sense of humor, Kate," he remarked, "because I've got one hell of a black temper and I'm not in the least embarrassed about losing it. I'm impatient and bull-headed, and I can wring you out like a wet cloth before you know it. If you tend to be a crier, you won't last here two days."

"Would you like to bet on how long I'll last?" she asked him.

"We'll wait and see about that."

"Whatever you say, boss," she teased.

She thought she'd seen big dogs before, but the gray shadow that rose ominously by the big chair in the den of the big cabin caused her heart to rise in her throat.

There was a soft, dangerous deep growl as she and Cambridge moved into the room.

"Stop showing off, Hunter," he growled at the animal. "Come here and try to pretend you're a pet."

"He's awfully big, isn't he?" Kate asked nervously, but she knelt and held out a hand for the dog to sniff, hoping he wouldn't consider it an invitation to a quick snack.

"Do you like dogs?" Cambridge asked.

"I like cats better, but I'm afraid of them. Dogs, I mean," she added as Hunter came up and sniffed at her hand. His tail started wagging and she let out a deep breath, not realizing that she'd been holding it.

"You'll get used to him. Here, boy," he coaxed, and the big animal came up to sit at his feet, nuzzling contentedly. "He was just a pet until I had the accident," he explained. "Now, he's my eyes most of the time."

"You didn't have him with you yesterday."

"I was trying something new... navigating without aids." He chuckled. "Not very successfully, I have to admit. Yama finally did come after me. Nagging, as usual."

"I guess it beats having a wife nag you. Or, are you married?" she asked, remembering that she wasn't supposed to know anything about him.

A shadow passed over his face and his eyes glittered like green fires for an instant. "No," he growled, "I'm not married."

"I'm sorry," she said, placing an

apologetic hand on his sleeve, "I didn't mean to pry."

The light contact seemed to make him stiffen even more, and she quickly removed her hand. He didn't like to be touched, that was apparent, and she mentally filed that fact for future reference.

"How soon do you want me to start?" Kate asked quietly.

"Tomorrow."

"So soon? But I'll need to pack, and get in touch with my father..."

"You can call him from here," he told her.

"But he lives in Austin, Texas... well not exactly in it, but as near as not!" she protested.

"Kate, I'm not a poor man," he said quietly, drawing on the cigarette in his hand. "You're bound to find that out sooner or later. I'm as prone to sudden whims as a politician is to platform changes. You may wake up in the morning and find yourself on a plane to the Bahamas. I'm restless and I like to travel and I've got the wealth to make it feasible. One long distance phone call isn't likely to break me." He turned toward where he thought she should be. "Are you afraid of planes?"

"Why...no," she admitted.

"Are you afraid of traveling?"

"I've never done much of it...."

"Is your passport in order?"

"But I haven't got one, I've never...."

"It doesn't matter, I'll have Pattie take care of it," he said. He frowned at her silence. "Pattie," he emphasized, "is my office secretary. She's young, enthusiastic, and disgustingly efficient."

"And madly in love with the boss, I'll bet," she taunted.

"God, I hope not! She's married to one of my assistant vice presidents."

"Oh," she said.

He smiled. "Sorry to disillusion you, honey, but I don't seduce the office staff."

She blushed furiously. "I'd better go home and start packing," she said, watching the way his big hand was ruffling the dog's soft fur.

"Don't take too much time. I've been idle long enough. I want to get my mind back on something constructive."

She felt a twinge of conscience. "Of course. I won't be long."

She brooded while she packed, praying that she was doing the right thing. There were so many pitfalls. What if his memory came back and somebody described her to him, wouldn't he remember what she looked like? What if…?

She forced herself to stop thinking about it. Tomorrow would take care of tomorrow, and worrying wasn't going to change anything. Besides, it was time she stopped thinking about herself and started thinking about someone else. It was just beginning to occur to her that she'd done very little of that in recent months. She'd been too buried in bitterness and self-pity to turn her thoughts outward at all. Perhaps it would be good therapy, working for someone like Garet Cambridge. He wasn't the kind of man to tolerate self-pity in any form, even his own.

He puzzled her. She'd never known anyone quite like him, and despite his wealth and her lack of it, she felt a strange kinship with him. He made her comfortable with herself and the world around her. He made her feel somehow secure and protected. Perhaps he, too, needed companionship for a little while. Someone to make his path a little easier. If only, she thought, she hadn't made the path so rough for him in the first place!

She sent Maude a telegram before she left the cottage, and that night she called her father from her new bedroom in Cambridge's spacious beach house.

"I thought you might get home for a visit between jobs," her father chuckled. "No hope, I guess."

"I'll make it next month, I promise," she said. "Oh, Dad, I've been such a pill, and I'm so sorry! I'm going to make it all up to you, I promise."

"Kate," he said gently, "you're my best girl and I love you. Don't feel you owe me anything."

"But I do! I do! All those years you put in on me when I was growing up, after Mama left, all the sacrifices you made...and for what? So I could run off half cocked with a status-seeking meat packer and leave you with a mortgage you can't pay...."

"Now, hush," he scolded. "I made the payment all right. I sold some of the cattle and got a handsome deal. I'm doing just fine, and you can stop sending me so much of your check. I don't need it now.''

''But, Dad....''

''No buts, daughter, I wouldn't lie to you. I'm not about to starve.'' He paused for an instant, and she could almost see the lines in his thin, leathery face. ''Kate, are you happy, are you getting over it?''

''I'm...just fine,'' she lied, feeling tears prick at her eyes. ''Honest I am. Will you write me if I give you the address?''

''You know I'm not much on writing, but you send me a letter first and I just might answer it, all right?''

''All right, Daddy, I love you,'' she said tightly.

''I love you, too, girl. Be happy, Kate. Life's so short.''

''I will. You, too. Dad, are you doing okay?'' she asked suddenly.

"Just fine, honey," he said. "You say about another month before you get here? I'll do my best to wait for you. I was going on a cruise to Europe, you know, but if that was a promise...."

"Oh, Dad," she laughed through her tears. "Yes, just a month or so, and please cancel your cruise."

"I'll see what I can do. Good night, child."

"Good night, Daddy."

Working for Garet Cambridge was like nothing she'd ever experienced. He was impatient, demanding, and utterly a perfectionist; but at the same time, he made the work so interesting that she didn't have time to get bored.

Before her stunned eyes, the book began to take shape as he roughed out the first draft and an outline, and her heart came into her throat when she realized that he'd actually done the things he was writing about.

"What's wrong?" he asked at one point, relaxed in his padded armchair with one brow raised curiously. "I can't imagine a woman being as quiet as you are today without some reason."

"Shell shock," she teased, glancing at the pantherish look of his big body in the armchair that seemed to fit perfectly the contours of that body.

"From what?" he asked, and his heavy brows drew together.

"Your life. Here," she added, glancing down at the paragraph that dealt with a plane whose engine caught fire and was forced down. "This part, where the engine burned and you had to bring the plane down in a swamp."

He smiled. "I brought it in between two trees and tore the wings off. That was a close one."

"It really happened, didn't it?" she asked.

"Yes, little one. It really happened.'' He looked thoughtful. ''I'd been going for eighteen hours straight when I got into that plane. It was the dumbest move I ever made. But the board of directors were waiting for a test before they approved construction. They had to know if the plane was skyworthy.'' He shrugged. ''There was a small fault in the engine design that gave it the tendency to short out and burn after the first few minutes of use. We corrected the malfunction and put it into production. It was our best selling executive jet for four years.''

''Do you want to put that in?'' she asked him.

''Might as well. Kate, how does it read?'' he asked, suddenly intent as he leaned forward to stare with unseeing eyes in the direction of her voice. ''Is it comprehensible to a lay person?''

''It is to me, and I don't know anything about airplanes.''

''I have a feeling,'' he murmured

with a half smile, "that airplanes aren't the only things you're ignorant about."

"How would you know?"

"Never mind." He leaned back again. "Ready for more, milkmaid?"

"Any time, Boss," she said lightly.

He liked the beach. Leaving Yama to tend the house and listen for the phone, she helped Garet down to the pier every evening, where they sat on chaise lounges and listened to the dark quiet sounds of night for hours on end.

"God, I love it here," he said on one of their better evenings. "I'd forgotten how quiet the night could be."

"Didn't you ever sit outside and listen to crickets?" she teased, glancing at him where he lazed back in the floral chaise with his blue shirt unbuttoned, baring his bronzed muscular chest, and his white shorts revealing his powerful, hair-covered thighs.

"Honey, I didn't know there was an outside," he replied as he sipped his whiskey sour idly. "You know what my life was like. I seem to have mentioned it a time or two."

"Cocktail parties, business meetings, phones that never stopped ringing...have I got it?" she asked.

"In a nutshell. Not much of an existence, but it was all I knew. Until now."

She lowered her eyes to her lap, her hands just visible in the yellow light from the cabin. "I'm sorry you had to find out...this way."

He drew a long breath. "So am I, honey. Blindness is hell to try and live with. But I've slowed down enough to get a new perspective on life. I didn't realize how much of it I was missing."

"Can I ask you something?"

"Fire away, Kate."

"You mentioned once that you needed the element of danger...."

"And you want to know why, is that it, Kate?" he asked in a deceptively soft voice, as his knuckles whitened around the glass, his body tensed. "What the hell business is it of yours?" he demanded.

She flinched at the harshness she'd never heard in his deep voice before. "I...only wanted..." she faltered.

"To pry? To pump me for old memories that are better left dead? You're just like every other damned woman, you've got to know everything there is to know about a man!"

She swallowed nervously. "I wasn't trying to pry."

"The hell you weren't!"

"I'm sorry!" she managed in a shaky voice. "Mr. Cambridge, I'm sorry, I don't know why I asked that!"

There was a harsh, throbbing silence between them, and she wished she could get up and run. But she sat stiffly on the edge of the chaise, her fingers gripping each other, her body rigid.

He took out a cigarette from the

package in his pocket and felt for a lighter, managing easily to put the fire to it.

"I told you I had a black temper," he said finally. "If you want out, now's the time to say so. But I won't have my personal life picked to pieces. Let's get that clear between us right now."

She pulled her pride together and wrapped it around her. "I won't ask again," she whispered, hating the tears that beaded on her eyelashes as she held back the muffled sound that would have told him she was crying.

"Pouting, milkmaid?" he asked in an unpleasant tone. "That won't work with me, either. It's been tried, by experts."

She drew in an unsteady breath and tried to concentrate on the night sounds, the soft splash of the lake on the shore, anything but the way she felt inside.

"I'm not pouting," she managed finally, in a voice that just barely wobbled.

He looked toward the sound of her voice, and his heavy brows made a line between his eyes. "My God, you're not crying?" he demanded.

She drew in a long, shaky breath. "Of course not," she replied.

"Kate...honey, come here," he coaxed, holding out his big hand, all the anger and impatience gone out of him as if it had never existed.

She hesitated, but he called her name again, softly, and she went to stand beside him, gingerly touching that warm, calloused hand. He drew her down to sit on the chaise, so that her hip touched his bare thigh.

His broad, strong fingers reached up until they found her face, and traced her eyebrows, her straight nose, the bow shape of her trembling young mouth. Then his hands swung upward

to find the dampness of her long lashes
and he frowned.

"Kate," he whispered softly. "I
didn't frighten you, did I?"

"No," she admitted. "But you...
you're such an awful bully, you walk
all over people's feelings...!"

"Do you have feelings, little innocent?" he asked in a low, sensuous
tone. His fingers went back down to
her mouth and traced its soft lines la-
zily, with a light, tantalizing pressure.
"I thought you were always cool and
collected."

"Nobody can be collected when you
yell at them!" she returned with a wan
display of spirit. "Please, don't do
that," she murmured, drawing away
from that maddening finger.

He chuckled softly. "Haven't you
ever let a man make love to you?"

She stiffened. "Of course I have,"
she told him with an attempt at sophistication.

"I said make love, not make out," he corrected. "You do know there's a difference?"

She blushed to the roots of her hair. "I don't sleep with men, if that's what you mean," she gulped. "Not," she added haughtily, "that it's any of your business."

"Before I'm through with you," he said in a low, menacing tone, "it may be very much my business."

"I'm your secretary...."

"God, yes, don't let's forget it for a second!" he said, mocking her. His arm shot out and pulled her down on top of his broad, unyielding chest. She gasped, stiffened, and tried to pull away, careful to keep her protesting hands on the cotton of his shirt, not to let them rest on the bare, cool muscles of his chest and the mat of hair where the shirt had fallen open.

She heard him laugh, as if he found

her unsuccessful efforts toward freedom some private joke.

"This," he murmured, "is unique. I
don't think I've ever had a woman
fight to get out of my arms. It's always
been the other way around."

"I can't imagine why," she panted,
still fighting, "unless they were trying
to get close enough to pick your pockets."

He laughed even harder. "You don't
think I'm attractive, milkmaid?" he
asked.

"No, I don't!" she flashed angrily.
"Will you let me go?"

He laughed, folding her even closer.
"God, you're good for me," he murmured against her ear. "Kate, how
have I managed without you all these
years?"

"The same way you've managed
without a pride of sons, I imagine,"
she fumed, giving way finally to lie
panting breathlessly in his steely grip.

"How do you know I don't have children?"

She considered that. "I'm sorry," she murmured. "I didn't think...."

He ruffled her hair. "I'm teasing, Kate. I'm not a father, to the best of my knowledge," he added wickedly.

"No doubt. Please will you let me up? I'm dreadfully uncomfortable!"

"Are you?" There was, suddenly, a new note in his voice, a difference in the touch of his big hands against her back as he shifted her gently against him until she was lying half-against, half-beside him.

"You...." she faltered as her hand came into contact with the cool flesh of his massive chest.

His big, warm hand covered hers, pressing it against his body. "Just relax, Kate," he said quietly. "We all need physical contact at one point or another in our lives, and it doesn't have to have sexual overtones."

"I didn't mean..." she began quickly.

"I know." He let his drawn shoulders relax back against the cushions of the chaise and lay there just holding her. "My darkness can get lonely, little girl," he said finally, and she closed her eyes against the pain of knowing that she'd caused it. "Lonely and cold. I haven't had anyone to hold on to. I didn't think I needed anyone." He laughed shortly. "Kate, have you ever stopped to think just how alone we all are? Separate, self-contained entities walking around in shells of flesh that hardly ever touch."

"Hardly ever?" she teased gently.

"I've had women," he replied, his hand idly stroking her long hair. "But never the right one. Haven't you ever heard of being alone in a crowd, little girl? Or haven't you ever been lonely?"

She closed her eyes, drinking in the

night sounds and the fragrance of his spicy cologne. Her hand, where it lay against the hard unyielding muscles with their wiry covering of hair, could feel the steady, hard rhythm of his heart.

"Oh, yes," she said softly. "I know what it is to be lonely. I think everyone does."

He drew her up, shifting her in his arms. "You aren't used to being touched, are you, Kate?" he murmured.

She frowned. "How did you know that?"

He chuckled gently. "You were so damned rigid when I caught you a minute ago. It was like holding a pine limb."

"You don't like being touched, either," she murmured. "That first morning I had breakfast with you, and I grabbed your arm...."

He laughed. "I remember. But that

was because of the blindness, Kate. It's disorienting to have people clutch at you when you can't see it coming." He frowned. "It takes some getting used to, this dark world."

"I'm sorry," she whispered.

"Why? It's not your fault," he growled, and she felt the guilt all the way to her toes. His chest lifted in a heavy sigh. He spread her fingers where they rested against him and moved them in a slow, sensuous motion through that mat of curling hair. She could feel his breathing grow faster with the action.

"Mr. Cambridge..." she whispered shakily, liking the feel of his big, muscular body, the closeness that she'd never shared with any man.

"My name is Garet," he said quietly.

"Yes, but you're my boss," she replied.

"Does that make me a leper?" His

free hand pressed her soft cheek against his warm shoulder. "I'm part cat, Kate. I like to be touched and stroked...do you?"

She stiffened in his arms at that sensuous deep note in his voice, afraid of what he might learn about her, what she might learn about him, if this went any further.

"Please, it's late," she said quickly, pushing away, "and I have things to do."

He hesitated for just an instant, as if he was weighing the sincerity in her tone against the soft young tremor of the body in his arms. Then he released his tight grip and let her jump to her feet.

"I won't rush you, Kate," he said as he reached for a cigarette and lit it, almost as well as a sighted person could. "You don't have to be afraid that this is part of the job."

"I never thought that," she replied

with as much conviction as she could muster, standing at his elbow on shaky legs. "I...I know it must be lonely for you, and without a woman..."

"I had a woman," he replied tightly, "while I had eyes." His big hand raked through the hair that fell across his broad forehead, and he scowled. "Celibacy isn't one of my virtues. You knew that, I imagine?"

"Yes, sir. It's...very hard not to know it," she replied.

"Oh?" One dark eyebrow lifted, and the fierce black mood seemed to leave him. "How?"

She read that amused inflection, and found her temper pricked by it. "I've got some correspondence to catch up on. Good night, sir," she said without answering the bald question.

"Elusive little cat," he murmured. "I'll catch you one day."

And wish you hadn't, she thought miserably. The memory of the boat

colliding with that proud head haunted
her as she walked back to the beach
house. The woman he'd mentioned he
had while he still had his sight...had
the loss of her embittered him so? That
would be another black mark against
her if he ever found out his secretary's
real identity. And, remembering the
blazing black temper she'd seen for the
first time tonight, she shuddered at
what the discovery would mean.

Four

It didn't take Kate long to discover that her new boss was a lonely man. It clung to his darkness like a second skin, a fierce kind of loneliness that made deep lines in his face, narrowed his unseeing green eyes. She wondered if the mysterious woman he'd mentioned, the one who'd run out on him, had been responsible, but she wouldn't dared to have asked. One glimpse of his temper had been enough to convince her not to pry into his personal life again.

Even though he couldn't see, she sensed sometimes that he knew she watched him. She couldn't help it. His dark masculinity drew her eyes like a magnet—the bigness of his husky frame, the proud carriage that didn't falter even in blindness.

The only thing that seemed to dent his proud spirit were the headaches. They came in the night, and she'd hear him pacing his room, back and forth, in the early hours of morning. It made her guilt even worse, because more often than not he suffered in silence. Only on rare occasions would he call for her to bring him something for the pain.

"Have you told the doctor about these headaches?" Kate asked him early in the darkness of the morning while she was handing him two pain capsules.

"What the hell could he do?" he growled as he swallowed them down. "Sympathize? Give me more of these damned painkillers? If he's such a magician, Kate, why the hell can't he give me back my sight? Oh, God, if I could just see…!"

The anguish in his voice brought her a kind of pain she'd never experienced. Without thinking, she sat down on the bed beside him and wrapped her slender arms around him, holding him to her, rocking him in the stillness.

"I'm sorry, I'm sorry," she whispered, crooning like a mother for a lost child. "I'm so sorry."

He drew a deep, shuddering breath and crushed her against his husky body for just an instant before he pushed her away.

"Don't, Kate," he said quietly. "I might just mistake that well-placed sympathy for an invitation, and then where would you be? I don't have to tell you how long I've been without a woman, and Yama's not likely to interrupt us.''

''I only meant to offer you sympathy—not myself,'' she said in a small, tight voice, hating the naivete responsible for the hot blush of her cheeks.

''I know that. But you don't know what goes on inside a man's head when he feels a soft young body against him,'' he replied. ''Light me a cigarette, honey.''

She complied with shaking hands and put it to his firm, chiseled lips with their shadow of surrounding beard. Unshaven, he had a roguish look that suited him.

''Were any of your ancestors pirates?'' she asked without thinking.

He laughed, putting a hand to his temples as if the sound had aggravated the pain. ''What brought that on?''

"I don't know. Without a fresh shave, you kind of reminded me of Henry Morgan."

One dark eyebrow went up. "I didn't realize you were old enough to have known him."

"I've seen pictures."

"They didn't have cameras on pirate ships."

"There was a movie…!"

"With an actor playing a part, and it's the actor I remind you of, not the pirate. Now, isn't that so?" he challenged.

She sighed furiously. "It would be easier to argue with a stone wall!" she burst out.

"Damned straight, you might have a chance of winning." He took a long draw from the cigarette and sighed. "God, it hurts."

Her hand laid gently on his big arm, feeling the hard muscle through the silky pajama top that hung loose over his chest. It was burgundy, and emphasized the darkness of his complexion.

He covered that small, cold hand with one of his. "Stay with me for a while, Kate," he said quietly. "Keep my ghosts at bay while these pills have a chance to work."

Her fingers contracted against his arm. "Do you have ghosts?"

"Don't we all? Don't you?" he asked.

She sighed. "Oh, yes. I have one of my own."

"How big?"

She shrugged. "I hurt someone very much," she admitted, "because of my own stupidity. And there's no way I can ever make it up."

His big hand caught hers where it lay on his arm. "Don't try to live in the past. It's hard enough when you take one day at a time."

"Sage words," she smiled.

"And easier said than done, right, Kate?" he asked quietly.

"Yes, sir."

He caught her small hand and drew it to his chest. "Light me another cigarette, honey."

She took the finished butt from his hand and put it in the ashtray, lighting another for him. She had to do it with one hand, because he didn't show any inclination to let go of the one he held captive. She placed the filter tip between his chiseled lips.

"You smoke too much," she accused softly.

"Don't lecture me."

"Is the pain easing off any?"

He drew in a deep breath. "Some."

Her fingers contracted around his, feeling the warm strength in them. "I'm sorry about the headache."

He laughed shortly as he took a draw from the cigarette. "That makes two of us. Your hands are cold, little one.''

''I'm chilly,'' she said quickly.

''In the middle of summer?'' he teased lightly. ''I don't think so.''

''I am!''

''It's like arguing with a wall, Kate,'' he reminded her, ''and you know you won't win. Why are you so nervous near me?''

Now there, she thought miserably, was a dandy question. ''Well...'' she murmured.

''I'm sorry I tore into you the other night,'' he told her, with genuine regret in his deep, measured voice. ''I...'' He took a long, slow breath. ''There was a woman, Kate.'' His hand contracted around hers painfully. ''I suppose it was the closest I've ever come to loving anyone. When this happened,'' he gestured toward his eyes, ''she walked out on me. I told her the blindness was probably only temporary, but she wasn't willing to take the chance. The world is too big, she said, to let herself be tied down to a cripple.'' His jaw tautened with the hated word. His fingers were crushing hers now, and she grimaced and moaned with the pain. ''My God, I'm sorry!'' he said quickly, releasing his unconsciously cruel grip to caress the fingers his had punished. ''I didn't mean to do that, Kate. Did I hurt you badly?''

She swallowed back the tears. ''It's...all right.''

''Is it?'' His blind eyes stared toward the sound of her voice, a dark, emerald green against the darkness of his face with its leonine contours. ''God, I wish I could see you! I can't even tell if you're lying to me.''

She blanched at the thought that even the blindness was her fault. ''I really am all right,'' she said reassuringly.

He laid back against the pillows

with a heavy sigh. "I'm not a gentle man by nature, Kate. It's another of my faults you'll have to adapt to."

"Along with your green warts and your amusing temper?" she asked, tongue-in-cheek.

The black mood seemed to drop from him and he grinned reluctantly. "Think you're cute, don't you?"

"I have a sterling self-image, thanks," she laughed.

He chuckled, a soft, pleasant sound in the soft light of the bedroom. "You're good for me."

"I won't let you feel sorry for yourself. It goes contrary to your nature, anyway. You're not the kind of man to turn to self-pity, no matter what happens to you."

He drew her hand to his mouth and kissed the soft palm slowly, sensuously, in a way that made her knees go weak. "Am I?" he asked.

She tried to pull her hand away, but

he held it firmly, letting his lips travel over her slender fingers, against her wrist, her forearm.

"Mr....Cambridge," she whispered unsteadily, drawn in a way she'd never been by any other man as the slow, dangerous caress worked into her blood.

"Kate," he murmured, "put this out." He handed her the cigarette, clasping her free hand tightly, raising it to his cheek.

With trembling fingers, she crushed it out in the ashtray and started to rise. He felt the movement and checked it easily by slipping a hard, determined arm around her waist to bring her falling down onto the bulk of his hard-muscled body.

"No!" she whispered frantically.

His big arms wrapped around her, holding her, cradling her. "Don't fight me, don't be afraid of me, Kate," he whispered at her ear. "This is all I want right now. Let me hold you."

"Oh, please, you shouldn't...!"

"Why not?" His lips brushed the hair at her temple. "God, I'm lonely," he said huskily. "I'm so damned lonely! Would you deny me the feel of a woman in my arms to make the night just a little more bearable?"

She could feel the heavy, hard thunder of his heart against her through all the layers of clothing. "I...that isn't...all you want," she replied.

He drew in a hard breath and his arms tightened. "No, damn it, that's not all I want! I want you," he growled at her ear. "You, Kate! Every soft inch of you, here, now...!"

"No!"

"Why not?" he persisted. "Let me show you how it could be, Kate...."

He brought her face around and found her lips blindly with his, probing gently, teasing them with a pressure so light and unexpected that it took the hard tension out of her limbs and made her go soft against him. She'd been kissed before, but never like this, never in a way that made her feel giddy and boneless and hungry. The feel of his chiseled lips against hers was intoxicating. She parted her own to tempt them into hardness, to provoke that torturous soft brushing into something far more violent and satisfying.

She felt him ease her yielding body across his until she was on her back and he was looming over her, his breath mingling with hers as he held the slow, tender kiss in the burning silence of the night.

His hand spread against her cheek, his thumb brushed across her mouth roughly. "This can't be all take and no give," he said in a deep, gruff tone. "Damn you, kiss me!"

He crushed his mouth down against hers and she went taut instinctively until that hurting, angry pressure lessened and became caressing, tantalizing, seductive....

With a moan, she opened her mouth under his and slid her arms up and around his neck, yielding to him in a fog of dazed pleasure. His hands deftly untied her robe and she felt them on her waist, burning through the thin gown as he caressed the softness of her body and made it tremble.

"God, you're sweet," he whispered against her eager mouth. "I'll give you a night you'll never forget!"

Sanity came back with a rush at the words. She caught his hands and stilled them as they began to move upward on her body.

"I...I can't," she whispered.

"Why?"

She swallowed nervously, breathlessly, forcing the words out through swollen lips. "You know why."

He seemed to stiffen against her and

for a long moment there was silence, filled only by his rough, harsh breathing. "It was true, then?" he asked gruffly. "You've never been with a man?"

"No," she replied miserably.

He tightened his grip for just an instant. Then she felt him relax, felt his arms enfold her gently, with all the frightening ardor gone out of them.

"Just relax," he said quietly. "You won't have to fight me off, honey."

She nestled her face against his shoulder, feeling the sting of hot tears in her eyes.

"I'm sorry," she whispered brokenly.

"Sorry about what?" he asked gently. "That you had to stop me? Kate, I'm only a man. The feel of you went a little to my head, that's all. Don't feel guilty about it. I didn't hire you to keep my bed warm."

"I...I know, but if I'd said something at first..." she murmured.

"You're human enough to enjoy being held and kissed, little girl," he said, tracing her cheek with an absent finger. "You've been alone, too, Kate. Don't be too hard on either one of us." He reached over to kiss, lightly, her closed eyelids. "I like the way you taste, little innocent, but I'm not quite cold-hearted enough to make a meal of you."

She smiled in spite of herself. "You're a nice man sometimes."

"Sometimes," he agreed. "Kiss me one more time and go to bed. At the very least," he added teasingly, "you've managed to take my mind off the headache."

She kissed his rough cheek and started to get up.

He held her back. "Not like that," he said quietly, bending. "Like this...."

His mouth opened on hers, pressing her lips apart, exploring the soft contours of her mouth with a practiced expertise that brought a moan from her throat. He drew back with a wisp of a smile. "You've got a hell of a lot to learn about lovemaking," he said gently.

Even without his sight, he read her too well, and it was unnerving. She drew a sharp breath. "I'm very sleepy," she murmured.

"Coward." He released her. "I'd give anything to see you right now," he added with a tightening of his jaw.

She got quickly to her feet. "Can I bring you anything?" she asked, ignoring the rough comment.

"I've already had everything I need...for tonight," he mused. "Unless you'd like to crawl back in here with me, in case the headache comes back?"

"No, thanks," she told him.

"Afraid?"

"I most certainly am."

He smiled. "You flatter me, little one. Sleep well."

"You, too."

She closed the door behind her and leaned back against it, breathless, dazed. Something intangible had changed between them tonight, and she wasn't sure how she was going to adjust to it.

He didn't know that she was responsible for his blindness, and now, more than ever, she dreaded having him find out. But, too, he came from another world; a world of power and success and beauty that no ordinary mortal could fit into; certainly not a small-time Texas rancher's daughter. She reminded herself firmly that, with eyes, he'd never have given her a second look except, perhaps, to order her off his property, as he'd done when he came across her sitting on the log by the lake. Cold shudders wracked her body. This kind of thinking would get her nowhere. She was a secretary. She'd have to remember that from now on and not let her emotions get between her and the debt she was repaying.

For an instant she remembered the woman he'd lost because of the blindness, and thought how much he was going to owe her for that accident if he ever found out. Her eyes closed momentarily. Death would be kinder than his retribution—there wouldn't be any mercy in him for Kate if he learned who his secretary really was.

Five

If Kate had been worried about facing him the next morning, she shouldn't have been. He was all business, as usual, and there were no references at all to what had happened between them in the soft darkness. He was a little more brusque than usual as he dictated, but nothing he said betrayed that his interest in his secretary was anything but professional.

As the days passed, she noticed a new restlessness in him. In the middle of dictation, he'd suddenly seem to forget where he was and drift off into a scowling study. Finally, she dredged up enough courage to ask him what was the matter.

"What makes you think anything is?" he growled at her from behind his massive desk, his sightless eyes narrow, threatening even in their darkness, and she shivered, remembering the power of them before he lost his sight.

"I...I don't know. You seem restless," she said finally.

He ran a big hand through the silvered hair at his temples with a rough sigh. "I am—restless, bored, sick of routine." He leaned back in his swivel chair, and it creaked in protest under his weight. "Got your birth certificate with you?"

"My...Well, yes, I had to send for

it because you told me I'd need a passport...."

"You won't need a passport where
we're going; just your birth certificate.
We're going to St. Martin this afternoon. We'll leave here after lunch."

She caught her breath. "St. Martin?" she asked numbly.

"It's an island in the Lesser Antil-
les," he explained. "Half of it's
French, the other half, Sint Maarten, is
Dutch. I own a villa there."

"Where is St. Martin?"

"In the Caribbean," he said with a
half smile. "The bluest waters and the
whitest beaches you've ever seen. It'll
be an experience for you. For anyone," he added bitterly, "with eyes."

He withdrew into himself, letting the
bitterness darken his eyes more than
blindness had. Kate left him alone to
pack, wondering all the while if the
memories he had of the Caribbean is-

land had anything to do with the woman who'd left him.

Kate had never liked airplanes, but there was something special about the small Learstar with its jet engines and its luxurious interior. It made an adventure out of air travel, and its compactness was somehow reassuring when it took to the air under the charter pilot's expert handling.

Her eyes darted to Garet. He hadn't said a word since they boarded the plane. He simply sat there, next to the window, his face dark and brooding, his chiseled mouth compressed, his unseeing eyes staring blankly out the window under a black scowl.

Kate hadn't tried to speak to him, remembering the black temper she'd had the misfortune to run into once already. She kept her silence, but her heart went out to the big, dark man. He looked so alone—so terribly alone. Something inside her ached to reach

out and comfort him. It was odd, that
compulsion. She'd never cared so
much about anyone in her life, except
her father. Not even, she admitted finally, Jesse Drewe. It was a new experience, to care like that....

She jerked her eyes away from him,
as if she was afraid he might turn and
sense her staring with that radar-like
sense that compensated him for his
lack of vision. She couldn't start caring
about him. It was too dangerous! In her
own way, she was trying to help repay
him for the blindness she'd caused, by
acting as his helpmate for the duration
of the condition. But sympathy was a
far cry from the way she was beginning to feel, and she had to dampen
down her new vulnerability. He wasn't
safe to get attached to, and he could
hurt her.

Time went by in a blue haze. Before
she realized it, they were over the Caribbean. Yama pointed out St. Martin to

her, with its white beaches like tiny white ribbons from the height; its hotels and smoothly rounded green peaks and coral-colored roofs on dainty houses dotting the island.

"Mr. Cambridge owns villa on French side," Yama explained with a grin. "That because he never learn to speak Dutch. Too lazy. French accent is worst I ever hear, but it get him out of jail, maybe."

"Listen to the linguistics expert," Cambridge chuckled from his seat as the small jet received clearance from the airfield and nosed down for a landing.

"I speak good English," Yama protested.

"So did Tarzan," Cambridge muttered.

"You insult me, and wait to see what I put in front of you for dinner tonight," Yama threatened.

"Oh, God, why don't I ever learn to

keep my mouth shut?'' Cambridge
groaned. ''Kate, you make sure I get
the same thing you have to eat tonight,
or you're fired.''

''Yes, sir,'' she said smartly, but
with a conspiratorial wink at Yama that
made the small man's face light up like
a beacon.

The villa was delightful. Perched
high on a green hill overlooking the
white beach and its luxury hotel, it
stood out from the rest with its graceful
Spanish design and white, curving
walls. The stone floors were cool and
smooth and Kate wondered how it
would be to walk on them barefoot. In
fact, she kicked off her shoes just inside
the front door and gave a sigh at the
cold delight of the floor under her hot,
tired feet.

''What was that all about?'' Cambridge asked, turning to scowl in her
general direction.

"I love your floors," she said self-consciously. "They feel good."

One corner of his mouth went up. "Barefoot already, country girl? There's an arbor of bougainvillea at the back door and we're fairly well surrounded by banana trees and hibiscus. I imagine you'll like that."

"I'll like the beach, too, although I'm not much of a swimmer. Are we allowed to use the beach at the hotel?" she asked curiously.

"Since I own the hotel," he replied carelessly, "I suppose we are."

She flushed. "You didn't mention...."

"Was there any reason to?" He scowled. "Kate, money doesn't mean a hell of a lot to me. I've always had it, so I tend to take it for granted. It's no big deal."

"I understand. But you'll have to understand that I've been without it all my life," she returned proudly. "I'm not used to luxury, and it's not in me to take such things for granted.''

He pondered that for a minute, taking time to light a cigarette with confident fingers. ''Sorry you came?'' he asked finally.

''Oh, no,'' she replied quickly. ''I'm very grateful....''

''Stop being so damned subservient,'' he shot at her. ''I don't want gratitude from you, not now, not ever!''

She flinched at the whip in his voice, sensing that whatever was eating at him had nothing to do with her.

She started to apologize again, but quickly thought better of it. He wasn't in any mood for apologies. Something was eating at him like acid. It didn't show in that proud, arrogant stance, but it was in every line of his face, in the dark green eyes that glowered toward her.

"I'd like to unpack," she murmured.

"Well, hell, go do it!' he growled, turning on his heel. He turned toward the doorway and slowly, gingerly, felt for the door facing, the back of a chair, until he reached the long blue brocade of the couch and eased himself down. It was too bad, she thought, that he'd had to leave Hunter in the kennel. No way was he going to bend his pride enough to use a cane.

"Send Yama in here with an ash-tray," he said stiffly.

"Yes." She turned and left him there, feeling vaguely shaky inside from the attack. If he was going to be like this for the duration of the trip, she was already ready to go home.

But by the time she explored the garden and the peaceful stretch of land around the villa, with the blue Caribbean stretching out to the horizon beyond the sparkling white beach, she wasn't so enthusiastic about leaving. Islanders waved as they passed along the road beside the villa, and Kate waved back, feeling a part of the green paradise. It gave her a sense of peace, this slow, easygoing pace, as though she'd been running all her life and now, finally, there was all the time in the world to just live—no time clocks, no deadlines, no pressure—just peace and sand and sea.

Cambridge was already at the table when Yama called Kate in to supper.

"Where have you been?" he demanded irritably. "Hiding from me?"

She shrugged as she sat down across from him at the hand-crafted table. "It did seem like a good idea at the time," she admitted quietly.

He drew in a deep, short breath. "Enjoy what's left of today," he said tightly. "Tomorrow we start work in earnest. I want to get this damned book finished."

"It shouldn't take much longer," she said conversationally as she sipped her coffee, savoring the rich taste of it.

He nodded. He lifted a forkful of Yama's filet of sole to his mouth and tasted it. "Fried octopus?" he asked with raised eyebrows.

Kate smiled in spite of herself. "Filet of sole," she corrected.

He drew in a deep, slow breath. "Have Yama take you down to the beach after dinner. You haven't seen beauty until you've watched the moon rise above the Caribbean. It's a hell of a sight."

"Mr. Cambridge...."

"Why the hell can't you call me Garet?" he growled, throwing down his linen napkin. "Am I too old to merit a first name basis with you, little girl?"

She stared into her plate. "I don't think of you on a first name basis," she murmured. "You're the boss."

He sighed, and she could feel the barely controlled anger in him. "My God, you make me feel my age."

She didn't answer him, picking at her food with as little appetite as she could ever remember having. He was angry, and it looked very much as if he wanted a whipping post.

"Kate?" he growled.

"Yes, sir?" she asked.

He lifted his coffee cup in a big, steady hand. "I asked her to marry me in this villa," he said after a minute. "We were watching the moon over the endless sea, and I slid the ring onto her finger. I'll never forget the look in her eyes, the light in her face...I had eyes, and she wanted me," he said gruffly. "I shouldn't have come back here, but I needed to exorcise the ghost, and I couldn't do it on the lake. Bear with me. Can you do that, Kate? Just...bear with me until I can come to grips with it?"

"I'm sorry it happened like that for you," she said in a weak voice.

"So am I." He leaned back in his chair, looking darkly satanic in the subdued light. "She was everything I ever wanted in a woman. Beautiful, talented, passionate...her hair was like platinum—long and silky and thick, and she had the bluest eyes...God, I loved her! A month away from the altar, and this had to happen." He ran his hand over his eyes. "It's not clearing up. If anything, I'm losing what little vision I managed to retain. The darkness is gaining ground, Kate, and how the hell am I going to make it through life without my eyes?" he asked finally, and the pain was in his voice, in the hard lines of his face.

She closed her eyes against the guilt. "You'll manage," she told him quietly. "You'll manage because you have to, and you won't let it break you.

You'll go on, one day at a time, and you'll cope."

He stared in the direction her voice had come from. "Stay with me."

She swallowed. "I will. I'll be here...as long as you need me," she said softly.

"It came back to me today, Kate," he said heavily. "I remembered."

A nagging, uneasy suspicion began to form in her mind. "Remembered?" she asked faintly, gripping the smooth, wooden arms of her chair.

"How this happened," he said, touching his forehead. He scowled, and the look on his face was frightening. "That damned girl," he said heatedly. "I never knew her name, or where she came from but she liked to get reckless in boats and speed. I called her down once, but it didn't stop her. I was out swimming," he recalled, his jaw tightening, "and the last thing I remember is turning to see her at the helm of a speedboat coming straight for me. She didn't even stop, the little maniac! She didn't even come back to see if she'd killed me.''

Kate sat there like a statue, her face frozen and white, her heart beating her to death. She'd been terrified of this moment, and here it was. He knew. He knew!

Six

"That's going to be my number one priority," he said quietly, "when I finish this book and go back to the States. I'm going to find that girl if it takes me the rest of my life. And when I do, I'll crucify her."

He didn't raise his voice, but that made the statement all the more terrifying.

"How will you start?" she asked in

what she hoped was a calm voice.

"By hiring a private detective," he replied calmly. "I know she was staying on the lake. It shouldn't be too hard to locate her. I'll have Pattie get on it today. I don't want to lose her trail, not now. That little blonde assassin!" he growled. "If it takes the rest of my life, I'll get even with her for what she did to me!"

Kate's eyes closed momentarily. So that had been part of what was eating him all the way from Georgia. He'd remembered. And from now on it was going to be like walking on eggshells to live with him, wondering what minute she was going to slip up and give something away.

What if he started remembering that his assailant had been blonde, and so was Kate—that she'd been living on the lake when he hired her—mightn't he remember and recognize her husky voice, even if he'd only heard it briefly before?

She trembled at just the thought of discovery. There'd be no explaining away what she'd done. He'd never believe that it had been an accident. Not when he remembered how she'd defied him when he ran her off the lake, off his property. He'd be sure she'd hit him deliberately with the speedboat. Anyone, she admitted bitterly, would believe that, given the circumstances.

Tears gathered in her eyes. She'd gotten used to him—to his moods, his deep, quiet voice in the night while he dictated, the sound of his heavy footsteps, the smell of his cigarette smoke in the darkness. It would be hard to leave him. She hadn't realized that before, and it came as something of a shock.

"You're very quiet, Kate," he said, scowling. "Can you blame me for being bitter, for wanting revenge? My

God, I may go through the rest of my life like this, and all because of a child's deliberate attempt at revenge!''

"You sound as though...you think she meant to hit you."

"Of course she meant to!" he growled savagely. He caught a deep breath, wrapping his big hands around his coffee cup. "I'd run her off the lake once already when I caught her speeding. To make matters worse, I found her sitting by the lake on my property, and I ran her off again." His lips compressed. "Sassy little brat, she didn't like that. I wanted to pick her up and shake her. Instead, I let her go. It wasn't two hours later that she ran the boat over me, and left me there bleeding after I'd managed to drag myself out of the lake," he recalled gruffly.

"Maybe...maybe she was afraid," Kate suggested casually.

"I hope to God she was," he agreed. "Terrified. I hope she still is.

If I can believe that, I'll have something to live for!''

''Being bitter, hating won't help,'' she said gently.

''How do you know it won't?'' he demanded.

She drew a deep breath. ''Because I've learned it the hard way,'' she said in a subdued tone.

''The meat packer's son, Kate?'' he asked. His heavy brows drew together as he stared blankly in front of him. ''He hurt you pretty badly, didn't he?''

She sighed. ''I suppose he did. It hardly seems important anymore. I thought I loved him, but I'm not sure now that I even know what love is— or that I want to know.''

''I'll tell you what it is, little girl,'' he said softly. ''It's the sweetest madness this side of hell. When it finally happens for you, you won't have to ask what it's all about. You'll know.''

Did he, she wondered? Was it the

mysterious woman who'd deserted him that he was thinking about? And had it been remembering the accident that really upset him—or remembering the only woman he'd ever loved?

He finished his coffee. "Go with Yama. I've been on your back ever since we landed. You could do with a break from my temper. He's going to pick up some material for us at the hotel. You can enjoy the beach and see something of the tourist trade while you're there."

She swallowed down a little of her apprehension. Maybe his private detective would strike out, anyway. After all, Maude was presumably still in Paris, and the boat was safely locked away. She smiled.

"That's a first," she murmured as she pushed back her chair and stood up. "Admitting you've been like a bear with a sore head."

"I know my own shortcomings," he

told her. A wisp of a smile touched his hard mouth. "You're not still afraid of me, are you?"

"I think I am, a little," she admitted softly.

"I'm glad." Something odd flashed in those sightless green eyes, puzzling her.

"Sir?" she murmured.

"Remind me to tell you about it someday," he said. He leaned back in his chair. "Yama! Ready to go?" he called.

Yama appeared at Cambridge's side from the kitchen. "Yes, boss!" he grinned. "I take good care of Miss Kate, not to worry."

"You'd damned well better," Cambridge grinned. "I'd never find anyone else who'd put up with me this long."

"Pattie last good," Yama reminded him.

"Pattie," he replied, "has nerves of steel and a mind like a bear trap.

And,'' he added, ''she works by long distance, which she says is the only way she can get along with me.''

''I'd like to meet her someday,'' Kate laughed. ''She sounds like a girl after my own heart.''

''Insult me,'' Cambridge warned, ''and you may find yourself typing this book after two a.m. every day.''

''Sadist!''

He only grinned. ''Go away, little girl. I need my rest.''

''Naturally,'' Kate agreed impishly. ''What with your advanced age and all, you have to keep up your strength.''

His eyes narrowed. ''Kate....'' he warned softly.

''Would you like an iron tablet before I go?'' she persisted, exchanging an amused grin with Yama.

''Damn it...!'' Cambridge growled.

''We'll get you a shawl before we go, so you won't catch a chill in this night air,'' she went on.

"Out!" he exploded, rising from the chair with his face as hard as stone.

"Yes, sir!" Kate agreed, and took to her heels with Yama only a step behind, laughing all the way to the car in the driveway.

The beach by moonlight was everything Cambridge had promised it would be. Kate stood on the silvered sand, watching the moonlight play on the dark water, the glowing whitecaps rolling in against the shore, and wondered if she'd ever seen anything so narcotically lovely.

She stuck her hands deep in the pockets of her blue denim skirt and sighed, leaning back against one of the curving palms that ran the line of the shore. So beautiful, so lonely.... Even the tourists down the beach enjoying the sight from the comfort of lounge chairs didn't compensate for the terrible sense of loneliness that moonlit seascape fostered.

Suddenly, Kate remembered a night on the lake, a big, warm body drawing hers close against it, and a sweet, breathless shudder went through her. Why should she think of Cambridge when she was lonely? That didn't even bear thinking about! Especially now, with his memory back, when any minute he might regain his sight or recognize Kate as his "blonde assassin" by her voice....

"Worried expressions don't go with moonlight on a tropical beach, wood nymph," a pleasantly deep voice murmured behind her.

She whirled, surprised to find a tall young man in a pair of cutoff denims watching her. It was too dark to make out his facial features very well, except for a flash of white teeth.

"I'm Bart Lindsey," he persisted.

"Kate," she replied, taking the thin hand that was offered just briefly.

"Kate what?"

"Just Kate," she said cautiously.

"Mysterious woman! Are you, by any chance, a beautiful Russian spy?" he asked in a loud whisper.

"I don't think so," Kate told him, warming to his personality. "Although, I suppose I could have amnesia or something. What do you do?"

"I sell sea shells by the sea shore," he replied matter of factly.

"Do you have a sister Sue who does the same thing?"

"How did you ever guess?" he grinned.

"And do you have a white jacket with sleeves that tie in the back?" she wanted to know.

"I have one for casual wear, and one for dress occasions," he admitted. "How about having a drink with me? I'll even wear something decent for the occasion, although I'll have to admit that I prefer what I have on."

"Thanks anyway," she said. "But I

have a demanding boss who only lets me out for minutes at a time under guard. I'm due back any minute.''

''What does this tyrant do for a living?''

''He owns the hotel, among other things.''

''Oh.'' He sighed. ''So much for moonlight seduction. Okay, how about a rain check on the drink, in broad daylight next time? Even your boss couldn't make much out of that.''

He wouldn't care at all, she started to say, and realized with a feeling of panic that it hurt.

''Maybe,'' she agreed.

''Tomorrow?''

She grimaced. ''I'll be up to my neck in work tomorrow.''

''If I give you my phone number, you could call me when you're free,'' he prodded. ''I'm here for three weeks.''

''Well....''

"Be a sport. Say, yes, Bart."

"Yes, Bart," she said agreeably.

"Good girl." He drew her along with him back to the hotel. "I'll get the number for you and write it down. Too bad I don't carry my pad around with me on the beach; I guess I ought to in case I meet any pretty girls," he teased.

"You really carry a pad around with you?" she asked, noticing as they moved into the well-lit hotel property that his face had sharp features and his eyes were a playful green—as different a green from Garet Cambridge's deep set eyes as night from day.

"I'm a reporter," he replied, taking in her expression with a grin. "Don't panic, I don't do news. Just feature material, travel stuff. Right now, I'm doing a piece on the island. Fascinating place, part French, part Dutch, part paradise, and you can see the Atlantic

on one side of it, and the Caribbean on
the other.''

"How long have you been here?''
she asked.

"Today. You?''

She laughed, tossing her mane of
blonde hair. "Same here.''

"Something in common already,''
he teased. "Sure you won't have that
drink?''

"I'd love to,'' she said, "but here
comes my boss's butler now,'' she
added as she saw Yama coming out of
the entrance to the hotel. "I'll just
come down if I can tomorrow instead
of calling, how about that?''

"Suits me,'' he said with a ready
smile.

"If you're really sure....''

His eyes traveled over her apprecia-
tively. "Boy, am I sure. I shall sit
alone in my room and not move until
I hear from you, even though I may
starve and thirst to death.''

She shook her head. "How do I get involved with people like you?"

"You have rare good luck," he told her. "Good night."

"Goodnight," she called over her shoulder, and ran to meet Yama.

"You must not tell boss you meet strange man," Yama cautioned as they sped toward the villa on the hill. "He funny about things sometimes and I not like to see you get in way of his temper more than you already have."

"You're nice, Yama," she said genuinely. "I seem to set him off by breathing lately. It's his eyes, of course. He just can't adjust to being blind, even if it's only temporary. Maybe..." she chewed her lip, "maybe his sight will come back."

"Maybe whales fly," Yama said sadly. "Who man you meet on beach?"

"A reporter."

"*Hai?* Oh, no!" Yama burst out. "Boss kill us both!"

"Not that kind of reporter," she replied calmly. "He only does features about tourist meccas like this one. He was careful to make sure I understood that," she added absently, and wondered dazedly why he'd been so careful about that point. "Anyway," she went on, "he doesn't know who I am or who I work for."

"He know by morning, you bet," Yama said. "He ask questions until he finds answers. If he find out who Mr. Cambridge is, we both out of job, Miss Kate. Nothing boss hate more than press, and now that eyes no good...."

"He won't do anything about Mr. Cambridge," Kate said doggedly, "I'll see to that. Yama, I...I like him, and I need some company."

Yama smiled. "You nice lady, Miss Kate. Boss not sweet to you, but it hurt him all same if you leave. He think much of you."

She blushed like a schoolgirl. "He hides it well," she said with a little of her old audacity.

"He hides much. He lonely man, Miss Kate. Fiancee hurt him when she leave, and not first time. When they first become engaged, year ago, he catch her out with some other man. He take her back against much good advice. She not worth his little finger, but it hard to tell man in love that his woman no good. Now maybe he begin to understand what she really like."

"Was she very beautiful, Yama?" Kate asked.

"Only on outside. Inside, she ugliest woman I ever see. Hard and calculating. She like boss's money very much," Yama said coldly. "And he give her plenty. Only time I ever see him let woman get so close. Better he stay like he used to be, hard as nails."

She only nodded, remembering the side of him she'd seen that was ice cold, before she came to work for him. She shuddered in spite of the heat.

Seven

"Well, what did you think of it, Kate?" Cambridge asked when Yama had left the flat envelope from the hotel on the desk and retired to his room.

"The beach, you mean," she muttered. "It was beautiful."

"I'm glad you could see it," he said deliberately, turning away to light a cigarette.

"I wish you wouldn't be so bitter,"

she said timidly.

"Do you?" There was a low, threatening note in his deep voice. He blew out a cloud of smoke and shifted the cigarette in his hand. "I don't give a damn what you wish, Kate."

She closed her eyes. "No, sir, I never imagined that you would."

"Don't humor me, damn it!" he growled, whirling toward the sound of her voice. "I've had just about enough of that kowtowing manner of yours, Miss Priss!"

She bit her lip. "I'd like to go to bed...."

"No doubt you would!" He blew out another cloud of smoke. "But we 'old men' have to be humored, didn't you know?"

Her eyes widened and she stared at him. Surely that mild teasing before she and Yama left hadn't pricked his hot temper...or had it?

"Mr. Cambridge, I was only teasing," she said gently.

"Well, for future reference, I don't like that kind of 'teasing'!" he said roughly. He turned away and eased himself over to the open French windows, letting the breeze lift his dark hair. "I'm perfectly aware of my age."

"I'm sorry," she murmured, feeling a little like a whipped pup.

"Are you?" he asked harshly. "You sound watery, Kate. Are you going to cry? Scolded children usually do."

She felt the tears, but she wouldn't give him the satisfaction of hearing her shed them.

"If you're quite through," she said with quiet dignity, "I'm going to bed—Sir."

"Yes, I'm through," he said coldly. "I'd tell you to get out of my sight, but that would be a joke, wouldn't it?"

"Oh, please don't...!"

"Get out." He said it with such cold

contempt that she felt chill bumps rising on her arms, and she'd have given
anything to take back those teasing
words.

She turned. "Good night, Garet."

But he didn't even answer.

All night, she'd dreaded this morning. It came relentlessly, and far too
soon, and she felt every muscle in her
body tense with reaction when she sat
down at the breakfast table. Cambridge's mood hadn't improved. If
anything, she thought, shooting a
glance at him, it had deteriorated even
more.

His white sports shirt was open
down the front over the broad, bronzed
chest with its wedge-shaped sprinkling
of thick black hair, and she suppressed
a sudden, shocking urge to reach out
and touch it. Her eyes wandered up to
the firm, chiseled mouth, and she remembered without wanting to how it

felt against hers that night in his room.... What was happening to her?!

"Still sulking?" he asked shortly as he sipped his coffee.

"I don't sulk."

"All women do." He set the cup down.

She picked at her breakfast with all the enthusiasm of eating cardboard. "What time do you want to start work?" she asked quietly.

"I don't. Having to be shut up in the same room with you all day would drive me out of my mind right now," he said icily. "Go sit on the beach, and don't come back until you're through pouting."

"I'm not pouting!" she said shortly. She stood up, throwing her napkin down on the table. "And you go to hell, Mr. Cambridge!"

She ran out of the room, out of the house, and kept going on the paved road that led down to the hotel. Long before she reached the beach, she wished she'd worn a sunhat with her beige shorts and top. It was so hot that she felt like a broken egg on asphalt.

Without thinking, she entered the hotel, drinking in the luxury around her and asked the desk clerk if Mr. Lindsey was still in his room. He was, and she asked if a message could be passed along that Kate was waiting for him in the lobby. She sat down on one of the plush round sofas and waited.

She couldn't begin to understand Garet's strange behavior. For one mad instant she wondered if he might truly have recognized her, but her mind dismissed that thought as impossible. Still, though, what was the matter with him? And why was he taking it out on her, when she couldn't remember anything she'd done to antagonize him except that remark about his age. And why should that upset him?

She sighed miserably, fighting down

tears. He'd warned her what seemed ages ago that he had a black temper, and she almost wished she was back home in Texas. That is, until she remembered that Texas wouldn't have Garet Cambridge, and all of a sudden that prospect was as bleak as a desert.

She looked out the front door where the beach was visible from her seat, and she remembered what he'd said about standing at a window overlooking the Caribbean when he proposed to that faceless woman. She couldn't imagine that hard face softened with emotion, love in those sightless green eyes. Most of all, she couldn't imagine a woman stupid enough to throw him over because he couldn't see. He was so very much a man. Lack of sight didn't change that. But what hurt even more was the fact that he hadn't gotten over that woman. And Kate was afraid to think too hard about why it should hurt her.

"Well, hello," came a familiar voice.

She turned in her seat to smile at Bart Lindsey, suavely dressed in a pair of tan slacks and a patterned shirt that emphasized his blond fairness. "I hoped you'd be able to make it."

"I had to fight my way out, and I hope you're suitably impressed," she said.

He lent her a hand to help her up, his eyes lingering on her long, tanned legs. "I'm impressed, believe me. Have you had breakfast?"

She shuddered, remembering the scene at the breakfast table. "Just coffee," she said truthfully.,

"Come on, then, and I'll feed you. The cuisine here is *magnifique*."

"*Je ne parle pas Francais, Monsieur,*" she murmured demurely, flashing a glance at him as they walked toward the spacious dining room.

"*Moi, aussi,*" he seconded, and

launched into a monologue of French that left her breathless and protesting.

"I wasn't kidding," she laughed, "I really *don't* speak French—only enough to tell people that I don't."

He grinned at her. "I speak just enough to get myself slapped or arrested. I don't suppose you brought a swimming suit?"

She shook her head. "I wish I had. I...I left the villa in kind of a hurry," she admitted. "I didn't have time to put mine on."

"Boss in a bad temper?" he probed. "Mr. Cambridge's reputation is etched in stone here," he continued, smiling at her puzzled expression. "To hear the hotel manager talk about him, you'd think he was the resident holy man. Formidable, black-tempered, generous to a fault, rich as all hell, and the very devil with the ladies. Does that about cover it?"

"Just about," she agreed warily.

He seated her at a small table by the window and dropped down across from her. The dining room was almost deserted at this hour of the morning, but it didn't take long for a waitress to come and ask for their order.

"How about a continental breakfast and a side order of fruit?" Bart asked her, giving the order when she nodded and adding two cups of coffee to it.

She smiled at him over the dainty bougainvillea blossoms in their pretty vase. "How did you know to order coffee for me?"

"Because you look like a caffeine fiend. One can always recognize another," he added wickedly. He reached in his pocket for cigarettes and offered her one, which she politely refused.

"Pity," he observed, lighting up. "Caffeine and nicotine go together like ice and tea."

"So do nicotine and lung cancer," she said smartly.

"*Touche*. But I'm going to die of something eventually," he countered.

"I know, don't preach. My father says the same thing." She toyed with her water glass.

"How long have you worked for Mr. Cambridge?" he asked conversationally.

She eyed him with open suspicion. "Are you sure you're a travel writer?"

He laughed self-consciously. "Sorry. Force of habit. Asking questions is my profession."

"And ignoring them," she replied, "is mine. Especially when they concern Mr. Cambridge."

He eyed her closely. "Afraid of him?"

"He does have a temper," she said with a smile.

"What a waste," he sighed. "Burying yourself in an old man's memoirs...."

"Old man?" she blinked. "Memoirs?"

He toyed with the tablecloth. "Well, Jacques—the hotel manager, you know—said that he was a millionaire several times over. I wouldn't expect him to be a spring chicken. And you know yourself there aren't two pictures of him circulating. He breaks cameras, and reporters, if he can get his hands on them."

She laughed. "You wouldn't think he was old if you had to keep up with him. I imagine he used to go twenty-four hours a day...." She broke off, catching herself just in time. There was something naggingly suspicious about the questions he was asking.

"Used to?" He caught the slip and followed through.

"Well," she amended with deadly calm, "he is forty years old, of course."

"And you're what, Kate, twenty?" he teased.

She shook her head. "Almost twenty-three."

"Old enough to be your father, isn't he?" he laughed.

That had never occurred to her. She couldn't begin to think of Garet in that light, he was too utterly masculine, too vividly male to consider in any family sense. She could no more picture him as her father or a doting uncle than she could picture him with a cup in one hand begging on the streets.

"What's wrong?" Bart asked her.

"I was trying to picture Mr. Cambridge as my father," she said on a sigh. "I think I'd run away from home."

"Would you, really?" he probed. "I don't think so. A look comes into your eyes when you talk about him...are his memoirs interesting?"

She leaned her forearms on the table

and glared across at him, her pale brown eyes darkening. "If you keep this up, I'm leaving. Mr. Cambridge's private life is none of your business."

He had the grace to look uncomfortable, even a little ashamed. He grinned boyishly. "It's just my nature to be curious. But if it bothers you, I'll be the soul of discretion and not ask any more leading questions. Okay?"

The waitress came with their order in time to save her an answer.

Kate watched what she told him for the rest of the day—she couldn't make herself trust him anymore. But she did enjoy herself. Bart had a built in sense of adventure. He could make a mundane walk along the beach something new and exciting. He told her stories he'd picked up about dolphins and sharks and pirates, and pointed out other islands in the Windward group and rattled off history as if he'd been born there.

"How did you ever get to be a re-porter?" she asked him late that afternoon when they wound their way back to the hotel.

"Something to do with full moons, I think," he grinned. "Acutally, I had a little talent and I've used it to the limit, that's all. How did you get to be a secretary?"

"I could type."

"Talk about pat answers! But how," he persisted calculatingly, "did you wind up in St. Martin all the way from Texas?"

And that, she thought, would make a good story, especially if she mentioned her famous former employer and her part in Garet Cambridge's blindness. Nobody knew yet that he was blind, and what a scoop it would make for an ambitious young reporter. Kate decided right then that she'd never go out with Bart again. It was too dangerous. She might accidentally give Garet away. And she couldn't stand the thought of causing him any more anguish than she already had.

"It's getting late," she said, pausing in front of the hotel as she glanced toward the hill she had to climb to get back to the villa. "I hate to go, but...."

"I understand. The beast waits on the hill," he said with a grin. "Tomorrow? Same time, same place?"

"Maybe," she said. "Good night."

She turned and started up the road, her mind already on the villa and her moody employer.

Dark clouds were already blotting out the sun when she walked into the villa, nervously pushing back a wind-blown strand of her blond hair as she looked cautiously into the study.

"Is that you, Kate?" Cambridge asked from his easy chair by the window.

Her pale brown eyes were apprehensive, but her voice didn't show it as she joined him. "Yes, sir."

"I thought you'd decided to spend the night."

She linked her slender hands in front of her and clasped them tight. His dark face was as impassive as ever, but there was a storm brewing in the green eyes that stared in front of him while gray smoke curled up from the cigarette in his big hand.

"You did tell me I could spend the day, doing whatever I wished," she reminded him diplomatically.

"But I didn't know who you'd be spending it with, did I, Kate?" he asked in the harshest voice she'd ever heard from him.

She felt her face go white, and although there was no reason in the world for her to feel guilty, she did.

"How did you know?" she asked.

"People love to tell me things, Kate," he replied gruffly, his sightless eyes narrowing, his jaw tightening. "Especially about my private staff. You might remember that in the future. You can't make a move on this island that I won't know about."

She lifted her chin. "I haven't done a thing that I'm ashamed of."

"I know that, too." He took a draw from his ever-present cigarette. "What does he look like?" he asked in a deceptively casual voice.

"He...he's tall and blond."

"And young?" he asked harshly.

"And young," she replied deliberately.

"You're insolent, Miss."

"You drive me to it!" She took a deep breath, trying not to notice how broad his shoulders were, how massive his chest, how beautifully masculine his strong, broad fingers. "You don't own me, Mr. Cambridge."

"Are you sure about that?" he demanded. "Try to get off the island."

She felt her blood freeze. "Why would I want to get off the island?" she asked in what she hoped was a calm voice.

"Your boyfriend might ask you to go home with him," he replied coldly.

She blushed. "He's not my boyfriend," she told him. "For heaven's sake, I only met him...!"

"Time doesn't have a damned thing to do with emotions, Kate," he growled, as she could feel the tension in him. "One minute with some people is like ten years with others. And he's a damned reporter, too, isn't he? What a story he's sitting on right now!"

"If you really think I'd tell anybody anything about your private life, especially a reporter...!" she began hotly.

"Wouldn't you? He could probably persuade you to open up with a few kisses, or some cold cash," he added in a voice laced with contempt. "You did tell me once that you'd never had money, didn't you? What a golden opportunity this is.''

Something seemed to die inside of her, like a freezing of buds in an unexpected cold snap. ''You really think I could do that to you? That money means more to me than honor or integrity?'' She drew a deep, steadying breath. ''Is that part of being rich, Mr. Cambridge, thinking that people only do things for profit? Is it a standard that you measure people by? You're no better than that stuffed-shirt I got myself tangled up with! The only difference is that you're richer!''

His jaw locked, his eyes burned as they turned in her direction. ''That's enough,'' he said icily.

''No, it isn't,'' she replied in a voice shot with tears. ''But it'll have to do!''

''Kate, you aren't crying?'' he asked suddenly, his heavy brows drawn into a scowl as his sharp ears caught the difference in her voice. "Kate, answer me!"

"Why?" she wept, turning toward the door. "Aren't you through?"

"Where are you going?"

"To sell you out to the press," she lobbed over her shoulder, "isn't that what you think?"

"What I think of you would scare you to death. Come back here."

"Aren't words enough?" she murmured, leaning her forehead against the door as tears rolled down her cheeks. "Or did you want to beat me before I go upstairs?"

"Don't be theatrical." His footsteps echoed behind her as he followed, accurately, the sound of her voice.

She felt the heat radiating from his big body as he stopped just behind her, felt the tentative searching of his hands as they found her shoulders and contracted gently on her bare, cool upper arms.

"You don't know what's wrong with me, do you?" he asked in a strange, low voice.

"I think I do," she corrected miserably, shaken by the feel of his arms, warm and strong and exciting where they touched her. "It's remembering that girl, the one who hit you on the lake, and you want to take it out on somebody because you can't get to her."

"I'll get to her, Kate. It's just a matter of when," he said with chilling certainty. "Is revenge too violent for you, milkmaid, or does it shock you that I feel the need for it? She took my eyes, damn it!"

Her eyes closed against the guilt. "Yes," she whispered. "I know. But whipping me to death won't bring them back!"

"No, it won't," he said gently. "Kate," he murmured, his breath warm against the back of her head, "I hurt like hell. I feel as if my head's about to burst. Don't leave me alone just yet.''

A quick surge of sympathy and compassion welled up in her and she turned to look up into those unseeing eyes. ''I forget sometimes that you aren't...that you can't see,'' she admitted softly.

''Do you forget my age at the same time?'' he asked, very gently, and his hands moved up to cup her face. ''That I'm almost a generation older than you? That I'm too rich for my own good, and that I've got the disposition of a half-mad jungle cat half the time?''

''Mr. Cambridge...'' she whispered, pushing at his massive chest in token protest. Her hands accidentally touched his bronzed flesh where his unbuttoned shirt had fallen away. Involuntarily, her fingers tangled in the growth of curling dark hair.

His chest rose and fell more rapidly,

and under her hands she could feel the heavy beat of his pulse.

"Touch me, Kate," he said in a deep, tight voice.

Lost in the sensation of being close to him like this, drowning in the warmth of him, the tangy male scent of him, the sensuous feel of him, she obeyed him mindlessly. He was all firm muscle, all vibrant male, and there was a delicious intimacy in being allowed to touch him. Following an instinct as old as time, her face dropped to his broad chest and her lips touched him lightly, tentatively, and she felt him shudder.

His big hands tightened around her head like a vice and he jerked her face up to his blazing dark green eyes, eyes that couldn't see her.

"Don't do that," he whispered huskily. "It sets fires in my blood."

Her lips trembled as they tried to form words. "I'm sorry," she managed finally. "I've never done that before...."

"My God, don't apologize," he replied gently. "I'm trying to protect you, you hopeless little innocent! Do I have to remind you how long I've been without a woman?"

She blushed. "I wouldn't let you...."

"Oh, Kate, you'd let me," he whispered softly, pressing his firm, chiseled mouth to her forehead with a tenderness that was new and shattering. "You tremble all over when I hold you. If I started touching you, we'd both go up in flames."

With a start, she realized that he wasn't kidding. She was trembling from head to toe, and it wasn't out of fear. She swallowed nervously, enveloped in the comforting warmth of his body, drinking in the nearness like a thirsting runner. And as she started to analyze her tumbled emotions, it was like a puzzle suddenly fitting together. She loved him.

Loved him! A man she'd blinded, even though accidentally, a man who'd hate her if he ever found out. A man so far removed from her world in power and wealth that he might as well have come from another planet. But she loved him!

He felt the tremor that ran like quicksilver through the slender body pressed so closely to his, and his arms went around her to hold, to comfort.

"Don't ever be afraid of me," he said quietly. "The longest day I live, I'll never hurt you."

Oh, but you will, she thought miserably. You will, because it's inevitable that you'll find out who I am. And I wish I could run from you now, while there's still time.

"Would...would you like me to get you something for your head?" she asked softly.

"I've got all I need," he said at her ear. "You got rid of the last headache I had in a similar manner, remember Kate? Lying in my arms in bed...."

"It wasn't like that!" she protested, going red at the memory.

He chucked softly. "Oh, yes, it was." He tilted her face up and she felt his breath on her lips. "Kate..." he murmured. He bent and his mouth whispered against hers slowly, warmly, making her aware of him in a silence that seemed to catch fire. The lazy, deceptively comforting way he was kissing her made her hungry. Her nails involuntarily bit into his shoulders as he began to build the kiss, tempting, tantalizing her, until a soft, shocked moan broke from her lips. He knew exactly what he was doing, she thought dizzily, and if she didn't stop him right now, she knew what was going to happen.

She pulled against his slowly tightening arms. "Please...don't," she whispered achingly.

His mouth bit at hers with a slow, easy pressure. "Why not?" he murmured, a teasing note in his voice. "There has to be a first time, Kate."

"I'd hate you," she managed, her voice growing weaker as her knees seemed to buckle under her.

"Afterward, maybe," he whispered gruffly. His big arms tightened around her. "Oh, God, Kate, I could love you out of your mind."

Her eyes closed. If only he could love her, in the nonphysical as well as the physical sense—the thought made silver music in her mind. If he could love her as she loved him... involuntarily, she pressed closer to that big, husky body, feeling the strength of it against her with a sense of wonder, of pleasure that bordered on faintness. She loved him so...!

His arms tightened for just an instant

and then relaxed. He moved away from her, back to his deep armchair, and she felt a sense of loss, an emptiness, as she watched him sit in the wide leather chair. He looked older suddenly, and there were hard lines in his face.

"Go to bed, Kate," he said wearily. "It was a nice interlude, but you don't have to humor the blind man any more tonight. Tomorrow we'll get back to work."

"But, I wasn't...!" she burst out when she realized the direction his thoughts had taken. He thought her response was...pity!

"Get the hell to bed! You can't give me what I need," he growled harshly. "But if you stay here, I may ask you to try. I need a woman, damn you! Anything in skirts would do, but you happen to be handy, is that clear enough?" he asked when she hesitated.

She flinched as if he'd struck her.

And that was all it had meant to him! Those moments when she felt all of paradise in his arms, his possessive mouth, it had only been an interlude to him—something to satisfy a passing need. She turned and went out the door without another word.

Hours seemed to go by before she slept, and the phone ringing in the middle of the night didn't help her shattered nerves. There was something vaguely ominous about that splintering sound echoing through the dark villa. Something final, like a death knell....

When she went down to breakfast the next morning, she knew why she'd thought that. A woman was sitting beside Garet Cambridge at the breakfast table, her slender hand possessively on his arm, her eyes sparkling as she chattered away. She turned at Kate's entrance, and her identity was immediately obvious. She had curling blond hair and eyes the blue of a spring sky.

"You must be Kate," the woman said with a flash of ice in the glance she turned on the younger woman, and a smile that only touched her wide mouth.

"Yes," Kate said hesitantly, her eyes going to Garet, who was sitting quietly at the head of the table, his dark face giving nothing away.

"I'm Anna Sutton," the blond said. "Garet's fiancee, you know," she added possessively.

Cambridge stiffened almost imperceptibly. "Ex-fiancee," he said calmly, setting down his emptied coffee cup to light a cigarette.

Anna lifted a perfectly manicured hand to her short, curling hair. "Temporarily only, darling," she cooed, "just until you feel I've been punished enough for walking out on you, we both know that."

Kate sat down across from the newcomer and exchanged a sharp glance

with Yama when he brought her breakfast in.

"I didn't know you had a live-in
secretary, darling," Anna remarked to
Garet as she picked at her breakfast.
"Where's Pattie?"

"Still at the office, I suppose," he
replied quietly. "I'm working on a
book, Anna. I can't dictate it long distance."

That voice…Kate stared at the older
woman, and she recognize it all at
once. The cabin on the lake, when
she'd called to ask about Garet after
the accident—this was the woman
who'd answered the phone! And if she
recognized Kate's voice, it would be
all over.

"You're quiet this morning, milkmaid," Garet said speculatively, his
sightless eyes narrowing thoughtfully.
"Nothing to say?"

Kate stared into her coffee. "No,
sir."

"Docile, aren't you?" he growled.

"Yes, sir," she murmured.

"Have I missed something?" Anna asked irritably. She glanced from one to the other of them with a frown between her wide-spaced eyes.

"Only a few knock-down, drag-out arguments," Garet said with a hint of a smile. "Young Kate has a streak of impudence in her."

"Only when I'm pushed over the edge," Kate replied darkly, putting down her fork. "I'd like to be excused."

"No doubt you would, but just sit the hell where you are, Kate," Cambridge said harshly, freezing her as she tried to rise. "I plan to get some work done today. That *is* what I pay your salary for, not to play hookey with that damned journalist!"

Kate bit her lip to keep the hot words back, and the smug look Anna gave her didn't help any. She didn't like Garet's girlfriend. One look was enough to tell her that the older woman's only interest in him was his money. She didn't have the light of love in her pale blue eyes when she looked at the big man beside her. There was only a shrewd, cold look there, as if she was measuring the size of his wallet every time she looked at him.

But Garet couldn't see that. His big hand slid along the wooden finish of the table to catch Anna's and squeeze it. He smiled, and there was no mockery in it.

"Tonight," he told her, "we'll go down to the beach and you can describe the moonlight on the sea to me."

Anna leaned forward with a sigh, and it was a pity, Kate thought bitterly, that Cambridge couldn't have the benefit of Anna's low neckline. "Oh, darling," Anna breathed, "I'll describe everything to you. It'll be just like old times.''

Kate wanted to be sick. She wanted to scream at him. But all she could do was sit and pretend not to be affected.

''I'll have to get some work done first, however,'' Garet said with a grin. ''Make yourself scarce while Kate and I finish up the paperwork. Put on your bikini and decorate the beach. Tell Jacques to get you a beach umbrella so you don't burn that delicate complexion.''

''Oh, Garet, you remembered,'' Anna said. She took his big hand in both of hers. ''Darling, I'm so sorry about your eyes,'' she whispered brokenly, although there wasn't a trace of sorrow in her cold eyes. ''I'm sorry I walked out on you, it was just such a shock...but I'm back now, and I'll take care of you.''

''For how long?'' he asked conversationally.

"As long as you need me, darling," she purred.

Garet only smiled, feeling for the ashtray to crush out his cigarette. "Run along," he told her.

"Yes, darling." Anna got up and reached over to plant a sweet, long kiss against his hard mouth. Kate turned her head away, because she couldn't bear the sight.

Then Anna was gone, ignoring Kate completely, and they were alone.

"What do you think of her?" he asked quietly.

"She's lovely, and when do you want to start work?" she asked tightly.

One dark eyebrow went up and he smiled. "Jealous, milkmaid?"

"Of what? Your wallet?" she asked flatly, "because that's the only part of you *she's* interested in!"

Something like amusement flashed in his dark green eyes. "Not quite," he said softly.

Kate blushed all the way to her throat, almost knocking over her coffee cup in her haste to get out of her seat.

"I'll bet your face is redder than a sunset," he remarked.

"I never blush," she told him firmly.

"Of course." He got up, feeling his way to the door and along the passageway to his study, right behind Kate. "Someday, Kate...."

"Someday, what?" she asked

He stopped in his tracks, sweat breaking out, beading up on his forehead, and he leaned heavily against the wall, one big hand going to his head.

"Oh, my God...!" he groaned, and his eyes closed against a pain that Kate could only imagine.

Eight

"Garet, what it it?" she cried, running to him. She caught his big arms and stared up at his contorted face with horror in her pale brown eyes. "Oh, please, tell me what's wrong!"

"My...head," he groaned. His eyes closed tightly, and his hand worried them for several seconds before she felt him relax.

"Are you all right?" she asked, in

a voice more laced with emotion than she realized.

"I'm all right. It was just a pain, Kate," he said gently.

"No, it wasn't!" she said, a break in her voice. "Garet, you've got to see a doctor."

"What the hell for?" he growled impatiently. "So he can tell me to learn to live with it? I can't even see the blurs and shadows anymore! It's permanent!"

She wanted to sink through the floor. Her slender body seemed to shrink against his.

"Oh, is something wrong?" Anna asked, joining them in the hallway in a shimmering blue bikini with a towel clutched in one manicured hand.

"Mr. Cambridge is having pain," Kate told her in a cool tone.

Anna shrugged. "One of the unpleasant side effects, I imagine, isn't it darling?" she asked Garet with a smile. "I'm sure it passes. Well, I'm going on down to the beach, I'll be back in a few hours. Bye!"

Kate glared after her even when the door closed and cut her off from view. She couldn't remember feeling such a surge of unbearable rage before.

"Aren't you going to say something, milkmaid?" Garet asked, his deep voice amused even though the hard lines hadn't left his face.

Kate's soft mouth pouted. "Whatever I said would be either too much or too little. Anyway," she added tightly, "she's your business."

"Is she, Kate?" He caught her arms and pulled her against his big, husky body, holding her easily when she struggled instinctively to be let go of.

"Mr. Cambridge...!" she grumbled.

"A few minutes ago, it was 'Garet'," he reminded her smoothly. His big hands spread against her shoulderblades, drawing her relentlessly closer into an embrace that melted her hunger for freedom.

"A…a few minutes ago, I was worried," she said unsteadily.

"I know." His chest rose and fell against her. "I'm indestructible, didn't you know?"

She rested her cheek against the front of his brown silky shirt with a sigh. "I only wish you were," she said quietly. "I wish you'd see a doctor."

"You *are* worried," he murmured, as if he found the thought unbelievable.

Her eyes closed. "No, I'm not!" she burst out. "What should I care if you're too stubborn and hard-headed too…!"

Soft, deep laughter cut into the impassioned speech and his arms tightened. "Hush," he murmured. "Kiss me."

She felt the blush claim her cheeks and resisted, even knowing he couldn't see it, when he reached down and tilted her face up to his.

"Don't," she murmured.

"Kiss me, you little coward," he teased gently.

"Why?" she asked, but her eyes were already on the broad curve of that chiseled mouth, and she remembered the sweet, hard pressure of it with a sense of wonder.

"Do we need reasons, Kate?" he asked, suddenly serious. There was a strange darkness in the green eyes that she couldn't understand.

"No," she admitted, going on tiptoe to touch her soft mouth to his. "No, we don't need reasons, we don't...oh, Garet..." she breathed.

She felt a rough hand come up behind her head as he forced her lips hard against his.

"Like this," he ground out against her mouth, his breath coming unsteadily. "Pretend you're in love with me, little girl. Show me how it would be...."

Her arms went up around his neck and she threw caution to the winds. Her body swayed against his like a young willow as the kiss went on and on, a mutual hunger in it that was like nothing she'd ever felt. He cherished her young mouth as if he wanted nothing else in life but the touch and taste of it, his big arms cradling her tenderly. She'd never known that an embrace could be so gentle, that a kiss could be a linking of minds and hearts so intense and pleasurable. There was nothing of lust in it.

When he finally drew away, she stared up at him in a daze, speechless, too shaken for words.

His face was like stone, hard and quiet and utterly devoid of expression. But the hands that pressed against her back were trembling, and the heart beneath his massive chest was shaking him with its hard pulsing.

"Have you ever kissed another man like that?" he asked roughly.

"No," she admitted without thinking.

He drew a steadying breath and let her go. "We'd better get some work done," he said tightly, turning away.

She followed him into the study and automatically picked up her notepad and pen, dropping into the chair beside his desk while he fitted his body into the swivel chair behind it.

"Is...is your head better?" she asked softly.

A whisper of a smile touched his mouth. "You have a foolproof method of chasing my headaches away, Kate," he said gently, and when she realized what he meant, she felt her hands grow cold as ice.

"No comeback?" he teased.

"I...I shouldn't have..." she murmured.

"Why not?" he asked, and the smile faded.

"There's Miss Sutton," she said miserably.

"Yes," he said thoughtfully, scowling. "There's Miss Sutton. You wouldn't be jealous?"

She stiffened. "You're my boss, Mr. Cambridge, not my lover."

"I will be," he said quietly, and there was a wealth of meaning in the lazy smile that touched his chiseled mouth.

She blushed. "No, you won't!" she burst out.

But he only laughed. "Got your pad, Kate? Let's get to work."

Anna Sutton was brilliantly talkative at dinner, monopolizing Garet all through the meal as the vivid sunset filtered in through the French windows and gave the villa a coral glow. Kate picked at her food, hardly tasting anything. Her mind was muddled with thoughts that didn't bear sharing.

She wondered idly what kind of a game Garet Cambridge was playing. He seemed to be as infatuated with Anna as ever, but why had he kissed Kate that way? Was he just playing one woman off against the other? Was it some kind of revenge on womankind because Anna had deserted him?

"You don't talk very much anymore, Kate," Garet remarked suddenly, cutting into her thoughts.

She lifted her face in time to catch the venomous look Anna threw at her.

"I...I couldn't think of anything to say," she stammered.

"You aren't pining for the young journalist, are you?" he demanded suddenly, harshly, and the black scowl jutted over those sightless eyes.

Young journalist? She hadn't given

Bart Lindsey a thought.... "No, sir," she replied quietly.

"A reporter?" Anna burst out. "You're letting your secretary associate with a reporter?"

"'Date' is the word," Cambridge said darkly. "And no, I'm not letting her."

Kate glared at him. "I can date whom I please. You don't own me."

"That isn't the impression I got this afternoon," he said with a smug arrogance that caused her to blush furiously.

Anna stared at her suspiciously. "Is there something I missed?"

"You might say that," Garet grinned. "Is she blushing?"

"Like a fire truck," Anna said angrily.

"I...I wish you wouldn't," Kate murmured in a husky tone.

Anna frowned. "Your voice is so familiar," she muttered, and Kate felt her heart stop. ''I'm almost certain I've heard it somewhere before.''

''I don't see how,'' Cambridge said, finishing Yama's well-turned steak. ''Unless you've ever been to Austin?''

Anna shrugged uncomfortably. ''I don't travel in those circles,'' she said haughtily, ''if you mean cattle country. I believe that's what you told me your secretary's people were into.''

Kate wanted to throttle her, but she kept her temper. She had enough trouble wondering what minute the blonde might remember Kate's unsteady voice asking about Garet Cambridge that day on the lake, after the accident. What if she recognized it? What if....

''Is your headache better, darling?'' Anna asked him.

''Much,'' he said with a secretive smile, and Kate kept her face down so that Anna wouldn't see the blush.

It was later that same night when the phone rang in the study, and Garet picked up the receiver before she could get to it. She watched his face change as he listened, asking an occasional question, and before he was through, Kate knew with chilling certainty what he was hearing.

He hung up and leaned back in his chair, frowning thoughtfully. "How interesting," he muttered to himself.

She looked up from her typing. "Sir?" she asked.

He sighed and lit a cigarette. "Remember that private eye I hired, Kate?" he asked conversationally. "He's traced the girl."

Her blood froze—froze in her veins—and she could feel the temperature of her hands drop degree by degree where they rested on the keys of the typewriter.

"Has he?" she asked in a husky voice.

He smiled, satisfied with himself. "She lived down the beach from me;

for a while, at least. She's disappeared now. Probably scared to death I'd go looking for her if I lived." His eyes narrowed. "She worked for a writer—Maude Niccole, you might have heard of her, Kate, she writes romantic fiction. Unfortunately," he sighed, "we can't locate her. She was in Paris, but she left with her father and didn't leave a forwarding address. I've got her beach house under surveillance, though. If she comes back, I'll know it."

Kate sat there dying. It was all over now. When he found Maude, and he would, he'd know the truth. Her eyes studied him, drinking in the sight of him, so big and dark and arrogant. Leaving him would be the hardest thing she'd ever have to do. Tears misted her soft eyes. She'd have to leave, and as soon as possible. At least that way she could avoid the confrontation that would be inevitable. Any-

way, he had his Anna now, she
thought, he won't miss me. Tears
rolled down her flushed cheeks at just
the thought.

"You're very quiet, Kate," he said.
She wiped away the tears, careful
not to sniff and give herself away. "I
was just thinking," she said, schooling
her voice to calmness. "What…what
will you do when you find her?" she
asked.

"I haven't quite decided," he said
thoughtfully. He linked his hands on
the desk, flexing them. His eyes narrowed. "But I'll come up with something unique, believe me. I'll make her
pay in ways she couldn't have dreamed
of."

I already have, she thought miserably. I've paid in a way you couldn't
imagine. I fell in love with you, and
my punishment will be spending the
rest of my life where I'll never see you,
or hear you, again. And death might be

kinder. Her eyes traced the lines of his face lovingly, achingly. Oh, I do love you so, she thought.

"You think I'm hard," he remarked when she was silent.

"No," she admitted quietly. "I don't really blame you for feeling that way."

"I can't help it, Kate," he said. "I can't help wanting to get my own back on her. I'll have to go through life in this damned darkness, and for what? Because a spoiled brat pitched a temper tantrum on the lake in a boat!"

Kate's eyes closed. He was right, he was absolutely right, and the pain went all the way to the soles of her feet. But she hadn't known what would happen. She hadn't known him. If only she could tell him the truth, make him understand....

She sighed. He'd never listen. She only had one option, and that was to run. But getting off the island wasn't going to be an easy thing now. She had to keep him from getting suspicious. She had enough money, barely, to get back to her father. She'd saved it carefully. But how to get away long enough? That was going to take some planning. She might be able to get Bart Lindsey to help her.

"What are you plotting, Kate?" he asked suddenly.

She jumped as if she'd been slapped unexpectedly. "Plotting? Why... nothing!" she said quickly.

"All right, I believe you," he laughed. "Come on, honey, let's finish up this last chapter while I've still got a clear head."

"Yes, sir."

Kate didn't sleep. She couldn't. And it didn't help that in the middle of the night, there was one whale of an argument in the hall and the voices roared through the cool silence.

It was Anna and Garet. She could tell that without bothering to open the door of her bedroom, and Anna was clearly getting the worst of it. Kate couldn't make out the words to tell what they were arguing about, but it was loud enough to carry all through the villa. Then, suddenly, there was the sound of a door slamming, and for a few minutes it was quiet. Then there was the sound of the door opening, and slamming again, sharp, angry footsteps, and the sound of another door slamming. Then quiet; an ominous, strange quiet that was suddenly shattered by the sound of a yell. Kate jumped out of bed without bothering to grab for her bathrobe, threw open the door, and ran barefoot down the hall to Garet's room. She thought as long as she lived she'd never get over that sound in the darkness, that harsh scream of pain that echoed through the villa.

Yama was already by the bed when she got there, his face heavily lined, his eyes frightened as they lifted to Kate's.

Garet was as white as cotton, his eyes closed, his face strangely relaxed, strangely youthful looking as he lay there against the pillows. His breathing was shallow, erratic. Kate bit her lip, her eyes wincing.

"Oh, Yama, what happened?" she breathed, her eyes never leaving the still figure on the bed, as she stood trying to catch her breath, to cope with the fear.

"Headaches get closer together since we come here," Yama said worriedly. "He not say so, but I know him and can tell. It why his temper so bad lately. Miss Kate, doctor warn him this may happen if he not rest, and he have fall tonight after Miss Sutton leave. I find him in study and get him to bed. Not know if it cause this or not, but we must get him to a doctor, and quick. I call Pattie. She make arrangements. You stay with him?''

She sat down in the chair by the bed and took his limp, cool hand in hers, her eyes eating him. ''Oh, yes,'' she breathed, ''I'll stay with him. Miss Sutton...left?''

''Very fast,'' Yama told her. ''She upset him and he tell her to go. Finally show good sense, now this happen! I make call.''

She sat beside the big man, watching him breathe, willing him to live. If only she knew what was wrong, if she could do something!

Her hand tightened on his. Her doing—it was all her doing. And if he died, what use would living be, and that would be her fault, too. Oh, what a horrible day it was when she got behind the wheel of that boat and gave vent to her temper. She'd have given ten years of her life to undo it. She'd

have given her life. He couldn't die.
He couldn't!

It seemed an eternity before Yama
came back, quiet and solemn.

"Pattie calling doctor now," he
said. "I call charter pilot and he standing by at airport. Also call hotel, manager sending men up to help get him
into plane. I go with him, Miss Kate."

Tears rolled hot and wet down her
cheeks. "Oh, Yama," she whispered
brokenly, her hands grasping that big
one of Garet's tightly.

"It be all right," Yama said, awk-
wardly patting her on the shoulder.
"Boss tough. It takes more than this to
get him down. Miss Kate, I think it
best you come with us back to states.
Must refuel in Atlanta, can leave you
there to go back to lake house and
wait, okay?"

She could barely think at all, and
was dimly grateful for somebody to
tell her what to do. She only nodded

through the tears, her eyes never leaving Garet.

"He's so pale," she whispered.

"I know. You pack, Miss Kate. I stay with him."

"Yes, Yama." She got up slowly, her eyes showing the hurt as plainly as if she'd screamed it the width of the room. She let go of his hand, but it was letting go of life.

Kate hardly remembered the rest of that horrible night. Everything seemed to happen all at once. The hotel employees came to lift the big man onto a stretcher, and they transported him in a station wagon to the waiting Learstar. Kate sat beside him on the plane, holding his hand, her eyes burning with tears, her mind numb with fear. He was still breathing, but he hadn't regained consciousness, not for an instant. She'd never been so afraid before. If he didn't make it....

"He be all right, Miss Kate," Yama said from beside her. He handed her a key and a wad of bills. "You rent car, go back to lake house. This key. It be good idea also if you get Hunter out of kennel to stay with you."

"Yama, I thought I might go home...." she began.

"No, Miss Kate," he shook his head emphatically. "Boss do better if he know where you are. Also, Pattie and I can get to you better. Please, Miss Kate, not to argue."

She sighed. "All right," she said wearily, "I'll do it."

Besides, she thought, it would give her the opportunity to check on Maude's cabin. If Maude was no longer in France, there was a good possibility that she'd come back to the lake, anyway. And Kate was too tired, and too heartsick, to argue anymore.

Her eyes went back to the husky figure on the stretcher. Please live, she pleaded silently. Please, live, even if it's only to get even with me for doing this to you!

It seemed so long ago that she'd had the run-in with Cambridge on the beach, so many weeks since the accident. And in that length of time, she'd come to know the man behind the power, and she liked what she found. He wasn't the tyrant she'd thought him. He was simply a man; a very lonely man who was, despite his black temper, the only man she would ever love.

Nine

They landed in Atlanta, and Kate watched them take Garet away to a waiting charter plane with a sense of emptiness.

"I call you soon as I know something," Yama had promised. "He will be all right, Miss Kate."

"Oh, Yama, I hope so," she whispered as she watched the plane take off, shading her eyes with her hand.

"What will I do if he..." She swallowed on the thought and turned slowly away toward the terminal.

It had been a while since she'd driven, but she got to the lake house with barely an effort. Now that there was time to think, she wondered about Bart Lindsey and what he'd think when he discovered that she'd gone in the middle of the night. Not that she really cared; he'd pumped her for information pretty hard, and she still wondered if he really was a travel writer. But when her mind went back to Garet, so still and white on that stretcher, Lindsey went right out of her thoughts again.

She'd stopped by the kennels on the way and picked up Hunter. The big shepherd was actually glad to see her, whining and licking her hand and wagging his tail furiously. She opened the cottage door and let him inside first, following him half-heartedly. The cabin held such memories—of that first morning when Cambridge had asked her to move in with him—of that night when she'd gone in to see about him when he had the headache, of the morning he'd announced that they were going to St. Martin....

She turned, her eyes on the telephone. She picked up the receiver to make sure it was still connected, and was reassured when she heard the dial tone. She put it down again and stared at it. Yama said the specialist Garet saw was in New York. Had they had time to get to New York? Surely they had. Was he already in the hospital? What would the doctor do?

She put her bags in the bedroom and went back to get the groceries she'd picked up out of the car. It was going to be a long wait, even if it only took an hour or two more for Yama to call her. Every second would seem like hours, every hour like a day. She

wanted the phone call and dreaded it
at one and the same time. Oh, please,
let him live, she prayed silently. Please
let him live, and if having him hate me
is the price I have to pay, then that's
all right, too, but please let him be all
right!

She fed Hunter and poured herself a
bowl of cereal. It had been almost half
a day since she'd eaten anything, but
she wasn't hungry. It was just a way
to keep body and soul together, that
was all. Her heart wasn't in it.

The weather was misty outside and
there were dark gray clouds on the horizon, hanging ominously over the
lake. Kate sat on the porch where she
used to eat breakfast with Garet and
watched the shadows play on the lake.
Something in the rain was vaguely ominous, foreboding. The sudden ringing
out of the phone made her jump.

She ran to answer it with trembling
hands. "Hello?" she mouthed.

"Kate? This is Pattie," came a pleasant, soft voice on the other end of the line.

"Hello, Pattie. How is he?" Kate asked quickly.

She held her breath until she heard the reply.

"He's still with us," Pattie said gently. "Although it's going to be touch and go for a few days."

"Is he conscious? What happened? What did the doctor say?" Kate fired away.

"No, he's not conscious, and none of us are quite sure what happened," Pattie replied. "The doctor says the fall could have caused additional pressure on the optic nerve, and then he went into a spate of technical jargon about exactly what he planned to do, and lost me completely. All I got out of it is that Mr. Cambridge will live."

"Oh, thank God," Kate whispered. Her eyes closed and she smiled through a mist of tears. "Oh, thank God. I've been so worried!"

"Yama told me to call you the instant I knew something," the secretary told her gently. "He was pretty upset when he found Anna Sutton in the boss's apartment here. Of course, she made a beeline for the hospital."

It was like the end of the world. Kate felt suddenly empty and alone. "Oh," she murmured.

"I hear she bombed in on you at St. Martin, too," Pattie probed. "And that the boss threw her out. She never gives up."

"So I noticed." Kate stared at the floor. "She only likes the size of his wallet," she muttered.

"I know," came the reply. "And so does he, Kate. Don't think she'll fool him a second time. He isn't stupid—although he does occasionally give that impression."

Kate laughed in spite of herself. "I

noticed that," she said. "Is...is there anything I can do?"

"Yes. Sit right there and wait for him to come home," Pattie told her with a smile in her tone. "The doctor says if he does okay, he may be out of here in a couple of weeks."

"Two weeks," Kate murmured. She sighed. She wouldn't be here then. She had enough sense of self-preservation left in her to run, before that private detective made the final connection for her sightless boss, before he threw her out into the street. She thanked Pattie again for calling, and put the receiver gently back in its cradle. Then she sat down, buried her face in Hunter's silky fur, and cried like a baby.

The next morning, she took Hunter and walked down the beach toward Maude's cabin. How long ago it had been since she walked this beach and saw the big, solitary man standing on the beach and was ordered off in no uncertain terms. She'd never have dreamed that she'd go to work for him, that she'd fall in love with him. Fate, she thought, was unpredictable.

The cabin still looked empty, but two of the windows were open, and Kate caught Hunter by the collar and started toward the front porch, almost running in her haste to find out if Maude was really home.

She ran up onto the porch. "Maude!" she called excitedly.

The thin little figure who came running out onto the porch was a welcome sight. Without thinking, Kate went straight into her arms and wept as if she were a hurt child.

"Are you really that glad to see me?" Maude asked, rocking the younger woman in her arms.

"I really am," Kate sniffed, stifling the sobs that rose to her throat. "Did you get my telegram? I sent you one...."

"It didn't catch up to me, baby," Maude said apologetically. "Dad and I left Paris and I dropped him off at my aunt's on the way back here. He wasn't able to stay alone, although he's much improved...anyway, when I got here and there was no sign of you, I called your father. He told me where you were." She drew back and looked straight into Kate's misty eyes. "What happened?"

Kate moved away, wiping her eyes. "I hit Garet Cambridge with the boat and hurt him...blinded him," she said painfully, closing her eyes on the memory of that horrible accident.

"I thought you were working for him!" Maude exclaimed. "Why would he hire you when...?"

"You'd better sit down," Kate told her.

"All right, so sit down and I'll bring some coffee. Then you can explain it to me."

Ten minutes later, sipping coffee in the living room, Kate told Maude what had happened in the last few weeks. When she was through, Maude just sat there shaking her head.

"You mean, he hired you, knowing what you'd done to him?" Maude exclaimed.

"No," Kate replied miserably, wrapping her slender fingers around her coffee cup. "He doesn't know I was responsible. Once or twice, I was tempted to tell him, but at the last minute...."

"Oh, Kate, I warned you," Maude groaned. "If only you'd listened to me. Do you have any idea what that man will do to you when he finds out?"

"A pretty good one." Kate looked at her old employer wearily. "He's hired a private detective, and they've traced me to you."

Maude seemed to go white. "A detective? Oh, Kate!"

"That's right. Has anyone talked to you at all about me?"

"No," Maude sighed. "But it's only a question of time. What are you going to do?"

"Well, he won't be back for a couple of weeks. I've got that long to make a decision." She left her coffee sitting and got up to pace the floor. "I guess I'll go home to Austin for a while. I hate to just walk out on you like this...."

"Don't worry about me," Maude said firmly, "I'll manage. It's you I'm concerned about."

"I just hope he doesn't decide to take out his hatred for me on my poor dad. I've been a constant headache to him lately."

"Poor dad, my foot," Maude said. "Poor you, Kate, I'm so sorry."

"Why? I brought it on myself. If I hadn't tried to take out my temper in the boat...."

"That isn't what I meant," Maude said kindly. Her pale blue eyes were compassionate. "You love him very much, don't you?"

Kate met that level look and sighed achingly. "Oh, Maude, I love him more than life," she admitted quietly. "I'd gladly give him my own eyes if I could! At first, he could see blurs and shadows a little, and they thought his sight might come back. But now, even that little glimmer of hope is gone. He's permanently blind, and it's my fault, and when he finds out, he'll hate me. I can't even blame him for it, but I'm so afraid of what he'll do."

Maude went over to put her thin arm around the younger woman. "That fact that you stayed with him all this time, and looked after him might carry some weight. Kate, he isn't totally heartless, you know. He may decide...."

"I don't think so," she murmured. "Even if this hadn't happened, I

wouldn't have had a chance with him.
A man that powerful, that rich; Maude,
if he'd been able to see, he wouldn't
have had anything to do with me, anyway. Look at how fast he ran me off
his property that day.''

"My darling," Maude said softly,
"don't you know that those kind of
differences don't matter? Men like
Garet Cambridge make their own rules
as they go along. They don't conform
the way we lesser mortals do.''

"If only I'd stayed out of the boat,''
she whispered, and the tears came
again. "At least he'll live. At least I
won't have that on my conscience."

Maude hugged her affectionately.
"My baby," she said soothingly. "My
poor baby.''

And Kate cried all the harder.

Two days passed with maddening
slowness. Kate kept herself busy
around the cabin, working on the manuscript until she had it completely

typed and ready to go to the publisher. It would give Garet a little satisfaction to be doing something constructive, she thought miserably. If he couldn't test-fly his planes, or design them on paper, at least he could write about them.

On the third day, the phone rang, and she picked it up with a feel of impending doom.

"Kate?"

Her heart leaped at the sound of that deep, slow voice, a little slurred by drugs, but just as commanding as ever.

"Garet!" she cried, clutching the receiver like a lifeline as she sank down into a chair by the table the phone was resting on. "Oh, Garet," she whispered brokenly, "are you all right?"

"Calm down, milkmaid," he said softly. "I'm doing very well. How are you?"

"I'm fine, of course."

"Of course," he scoffed. "You're crying!"

"I've been worried," she muttered defensively as she dabbed at the tears with a corner of her blouse.

"So Yama told me. What are you doing down there?" he asked conversationally.

Her heart pounded wildly and she stroked the receiver as if she were touching his hard, husky body. "I'm holding down the fort. I...I got the manuscript typed and ready to go. Do you want me to mail it?"

"Go ahead. Then just relax and enjoy the lake until I get there." There was a pause. "Missing me, little girl?"

"Terribly," she said without thinking. She drew in a deep, slow breath. "I, uh, I hear Miss Sutton's been to see you."

"Anna? Oh, she's been her constantly. Bringing me flowers, boxes of candy." There was a pause. "Why the hell aren't you here?" he demanded.

"Yama said that it would be better if I waited here," she stammered.

"Never mind, maybe he's right. Pattie tells me you've called twice already."

"Yes, sir."

"Don't ever call me sir, again," he said quietly. "Not ever, Kate."

"I'm sorry. I didn't mean...."

"Oh, hell, I wish you were here with me!" he growled. "I'm no good at polite conversation. Kate, you're not alone at the lake house, are you? You've got Hunter, haven't you?"

"Yes," she told him. "I picked him up at the kennels. He's...good company."

"Don't go out alone at night. Promise me."

The concern in his voice made her feel warm all over. "I promise," she said.

There was a muffled curse. "The nurse is here with a shot. I've got to go, honey. I'll call you tomorrow."

"All right. Garet..." she searched for something to say, anything but what she really wanted to say.,

"Good night, Kate," he said quietly. The receiver went dead before she could find the right words.

Time seemed to fly after that. Kate lived from day to day for the late night phone calls from New York lulled into a sense of security by the sound of Garet's deep, quiet voice and the new note in his voice that sent chills down her spine. There was nothing personal in the calls, just idle conversation, but it was wonderful just to hear the sound of his voice.

During the day, she spent her time walking Hunter and talking to Maude. In the back of her mind, she knew the time was rapidly approaching when she'd have to leave. Garet would be home in less than a week. She needed to start making plans now, but it was so easy to put it off, to wait just one more day, for one more phone call....

It was late afternoon when she heard Hunter raising the devil outside the cabin. Kate had just finished grilling herself a steak, and she left it on the stove as she moved quickly to the front of the house to see what Hunter had found.

She walked out the door in her jeans and T-shirt and came face to face with a dream.

Garet Cambridge was standing at the bottom of the steps with his big hand on Hunter's silky head. He looked up as Kate froze on the top step, and his dark green eyes looked directly into hers. They dilated. His face went hard as stone. And she knew, without a word being spoken, that everything between them was over.

"You!" he ground out, and the hatred was in his eyes, his voice, the taut lines of his big body. He'd recognized her. He could see!

Ten

"What the hell are you doing in my house?" he demanded.

She only stared at him, drinking in the dark face above the beige sports shirt, the bigness of him, the eyes that, even hating her, could see again.

"I..." she faltered.

"Did you come back to finish the job?" he demanded, moving up the steps to glare at her relentlessly. "Or were you finally curious enough to come find out if you'd killed me?''

She licked her dry lips. ''I'm sorry,'' she whispered in a voice that didn't even sound like her own. She was frightened of him now, frightened of the power he could wield, of his hatred.

''You're sorry,'' he scoffed. His eyes narrowed, contemptuous, burning. ''My God, you left me for dead, and you're sorry?! What the hell do you expect me to say? That's all right, no hard feelings? Well, I'm fresh out of forgiveness, you little assassin! I want your damned throat!''

She flinched at the tone of his deep voice. Her eyes closed on a flood of tears. ''I...did call,'' she whispered.

''Why?'' he growled. ''Were you afraid you'd missed?''

She started down the steps, but he caught her arm roughly and dragged her around, hurting her in his anger.

"Damn you, I'm not finished!" he said harshly. He drew her up under his blazing eyes and tightened his cruel grip. He studied her as if she were some new kind of insect.

"Skinny little blonde," he said mockingly. "Little spoiled brat. Did it grate so much that I called you down about speeding in that damned boat? Or were you out to get even because I ran you off my beach?"

"It wasn't like that," she whispered, avoiding his piercing gaze.

"Wasn't it? Oh, God, I dreamed about you," he ground out. "I thought about you every day I was without my eyes, and how I was going to pay you back for it." He jerked her closer and she cried out in pain. "You're in for it, now, you bad-tempered little snake. Now that I know who you work for, and where to find you, I can afford to take my time. I'll let you sit and sweat out what I'm going to do. It'll give you something to do with your nights.''

Her eyes met his, misty with tears, pleading, wounded. "Please...."

"Please what?" he asked curtly. "Please forgive you? You little tramp, not until I even the score!"

"I didn't...!"

He let go of her abruptly, thrusting her away from him. She wasn't expecting it, and she stumbled, losing her balance. With a sharp cry, she went down, falling the rest of the way down the steps to land, bruised and crying, on the pine-needle laden ground at the bottom.

Garet stood there and looked down at her, not a trace of sympathy in his cold green eyes.

"And that," he said quietly, "is where you belong—on your belly in the dirt. Are you hurt?"

A sob broke from her lips as she dragged herself to her feet, biting her

lip to keep from crying out at the pain
in her elbow where she'd hit the hard
ground. She rubbed it gingerly, obliv-
ious to the bits of dirt and pine straw
that clung to her pale blonde hair. Her
soft brown eyes looked into his accus-
ingly, as innocent and wounded as a
scolded child's.

That look seemed to bother him.
His eyes narrowed. "Oh, get the hell
out of my sight!" he growled. "You
can't run far enough that I won't find
you, anyway."

She turned away, holding her arm,
and walked slowly down the beach,
blinded by hot tears as she made her
way out of his life. It was over. It was
all over, now.

Maude held her while she cried. It
took a long time for the tears to pass,
and the bruises she'd sustained when
she fell were already beginning to pop
out all over her delicate skin.

"Are you sure he didn't hit you?"

Maude demanded, horrified, as she felt the painful elbow for a break.

"He didn't," Kate said quietly. "I...I just fell."

"All by yourself?" the older woman asked shrewdly.

Kate felt the heat rise in her cheeks. She looked down at the heavy rug on the living room floor.

"You could have broken your arm," Maude grumbled. "Or gotten a concussion. You could have broken your neck!"

"But I didn't," Kate said calmly. "In a way, it's a relief to have it out in the open. I haven't slept a full night since it happened. Now that he can see again, maybe I can start to live. Maybe I can put away the guilt."

"Did he threaten you?"

"Not in so many words, no," she said quietly. "I think he's just biding his time right now until he can decide how many pieces he'd like me cut into. Maude, I can't blame him,'' she said when Maude started to interrupt. ''You couldn't possibly know the pain he went through, the mental anguish of knowing he might never see again. I had to watch it, and whether he knows it or not, I paid for what I did in those weeks I was with him.''

''Whatever you did, it doesn't give him the right to manhandle you!''

''He didn't manhandle me,'' Kate protested. ''I simply fell, Maude. That's all, I fell.''

Maude sighed and turned away. ''If you say so.''

''Maude, can I stay here tonight?'' Kate asked gently. ''I...I don't want to have to go back to Mr. Cambridge and ask for my things tonight.''

''Oh, baby, of course you can stay! And tomorrow, I'll go and get your things for you,'' she promised.

Kate nodded gratefully. At least

she'd be spared the hatred in his eyes that last time.

That night was the longest night she'd ever lived through. Sleep was impossible. She laid in the big double bed in the guest room and stared at the darkened ceiling with tears burning her eyes.

As long as she lived, she'd never forget the look in Garet Cambridge's dark eyes when he came upon her at the cabin. She'd never seen hatred in those eyes before. Even when they were sightless, there had been affection in them for Kate. All that was changed now. He knew who she was and what she'd done, and he wasn't going to rest until he made her pay for it.

Ironically, he'd never know just how fully she had paid for her own reckless behavior. How terrible it was going to be, loving a man who hated her, and having to go through life with only his contempt to remember as the years went by.

If only Yama had been at the cabin, she thought miserably. Yama could always calm him down when nothing else worked. But apparently, Cambridge had left everybody behind in New York. Now he was at the cabin all by himself, and she wondered crazily if he'd had any supper. Maybe he found the steak she'd cooked for herself. At least he'd have some nourishment. The thought of him coming out of the hospital with no warm meal waiting set her off even more, and she bawled.

Finally, when the tears passed, she tried to decide what to do next. The only alternative was to stick to her original decision—pack up and go home. Once she was out of his sight, he might put aside his hatred and go on living. At least he still had Anna, she thought bitterly. Dear Anna, who loved his bank account.

That was what she'd do. She'd go home to her father and start over. It wouldn't be so hard, she told herself. She could learn to live without Garet, it wouldn't take that much effort. She'd see him in every man she met from now on, but she'd just have to learn to cope. If he'd died....

She remembered the silent promise she'd made—that if he lived she wouldn't even mind his contempt, his hatred. She swallowed hard. He was alive. He was in the same world with her. Her eyes closed. Perhaps it was worth it after all.

She overslept the next morning, and the fog was already beginning to lift from the lake when Kate dragged into the kitchen and poured herself a cup of coffee. She looked down with distaste at her blue jeans and T-shirt. She'd had to put the stained, dusty

clothes on because they were all she
had.

Maude was nowhere in sight, and
with a feeling of anguish, she realized
what that meant. Maude had already
gone to see Garet.

She sat down at the table and sipped
her coffee. She wished she'd begged
Maude to leave well enough alone.
She could have cabled her father to
send her the plane fare home, and left
the clothes behind. She hoped Maude
wouldn't catch the same treatment
from him that she'd received.

"Oh, you're up!" Maude said
cheerfully as she came in the back
door lugging Kate's suitcase. "How's
the coffee?"

"It's fine." Kate stared at her
wanly, her pale face lined with fa-
tigue, dark circles under her soft
brown eyes as she paused, the question on the tip of her tongue.

"As you can see, I'm still in one

piece," Maude told her, putting the suitcase down. "If you think you look bad, my dear, you should see him. He didn't even give me an argument when I asked for your things."

"Thank you for going," Kate said gently.

Maude poured herself a cup of coffee and sat down across from Kate at the small kitchen table. "He asked me about you," she said casually.

"Oh?" Kate murmured.

"He wanted to know everything about you. Where you were from, your parents, how you came to work for me...I thought he was going to pass out when I told him your father owned a ranch outside Austin. Does he have some hangup about the cattle industry?"

Kate's eyes closed. "I don't know," she said weakly. But she knew what had happened. He'd realized that Kate and his assailant were the same person. When he knew that her father was in cattle, he made the connection he hadn't made when he saw Kate standing on the porch of his cabin.

"He asked about the bruises, too," Maude said, watching Kate like a hawk. "He wanted to be sure you were all right. You didn't tell me you fell down the steps."

"It wasn't important."

"He thought it was."

Kate got up and went back toward her bedroom. "I want to get the few things together that I left here before you went to Paris. I...I'm going back to Austin this morning."

"Are you?" Maude asked with a tiny smile.

But Kate was already out of earshot.

She was just putting the last of her small possessions into the open suitcase on the bed when she felt eyes on the back of her head. With a feeling of uneasiness, she turned to find Garet Cambridge standing in the doorway, looking darker and more haggard than she'd seen him since the first days she worked for him. His white shirt was unbuttoned at the throat over his massive chest, his jacket was gone. He looked as if he hadn't slept at all, and his dark green eyes were bloodshot.

He stared at her, wincing when she instinctively took a step backward as he came further into the room.

"I won't hurt you," he said quietly.

She bit her lower lip, feeling the anguish come back fresh as she remembered what he'd said to her yesterday, and how he'd said it. "What do you want, Mr Cambridge?" she asked in a husky whisper.

"To see how badly I hurt you," he said simply, and he had the look of a man who'd pulled the wings off a butterfly. "To make sure you were all right."

"I didn't break my neck," she said gently. "It might have been better...if I had." Her voice broke on the words, and he was beside her in a flash. A muffled curse passed his lips as he caught her up in his big arms and held her fiercely against him.

The tears came like a flood, surging down her cheeks, and she couldn't stop them.

"I'm sorry, I'm sorry," she wept against his shirt, "I'm so sorry! I've lived with it every day, every night, and in my sleep...I could see the boat hitting...I saw you climb onto the pier, and I thought you were all right...and I called, and Anna was there. She said they'd taken you to the hospital and you'd be all right, but I didn't know, I didn't know...!" she whimpered.

His arms tightened. Then he drew back to look down into her damp face, searching her eyes in a static, throbbing silence.

His hands came up to cup her face and his eyes closed while he let his broad, strong fingers touch tentatively, gently, every soft line of her face. It was the way he'd touched her when he was blind, reading with his fingers what, at that time, he hadn't been able to see. He brushed the tears away and bent his head. His mouth whispered across her closed eyelids.

His eyes opened then, staring down into hers. "Kate," he whispered achingly.

She bit her lip. "Don't hate me," she pleaded, pride gone to ashes as he held her and she clung to him.

"Could I hate a part of myself, little girl?" he asked. "Why did you come to work for me, knowing that I could find out about you any day? Why take the risk?"

Her eyes lowered to a button on his

shirt. ''To make restitution in some small way,'' she murmured.

''You might have told me the truth in the beginning,'' he pointed out.

''At first you had amnesia and I was afraid of the damage I might cause,'' she recalled. ''Then you did remember, and you hated me so, I was afraid to.''

''It wasn't you I hated,'' he said quietly. ''It was the woman I thought you were. If I'd realized you came with me out of guilt, I wouldn't have made you stay.''

But it wasn't guilt, she hadn't stayed out of guilt. And she didn't dare tell him that. She couldn't tell him she'd stayed out of love.

''I...I have to finish packing,'' she murmured, and pressed gently against his chest.

He let her move away from him, but his eyes held her as surely as his arms had.

"Where will you go?" he asked
solemnly.

"Home," she said. "Back to my father's ranch. I never should have left
it."

He jammed his hands into his pockets and his jaw tightened. "I thought
I might write another book," he remarked. "I enjoyed this one, and I'm
getting a little old for test flights." He
eyed her speculatively. "We made a
good team, Kate."

Her eyes misted over. She nodded.
Her slender hands closed the suitcase.

"You could come back to work for
me," he persisted gently.

"Oh, no, I couldn't!" she said
quickly, and her pulse ran wild.

"Why not?" he growled. His eyes
flashed fire at her. "Don't you feel
guilty enough anymore?"

She winced, and he caught her by
the arms, holding her in front of him

as he read the wounding in her tormented pale eyes.

"Oh, God, is that how you used to look when I lost my temper with you?" he asked in a haunted tone, his face contorting with the memory. "Kate, gentle little Kate, I'm not going to hurt you anymore. You don't have to be afraid of me."

"I'm not afraid," she said quietly, but her body was trembling, and he must have been able to feel it.

He smiled half-heartedly. "Are you sure? You're trembling...." The smile faded as he caught her eyes and read them. "You trembled like this the last time I held you," he recalled softly, his brows knitting. His hands tightened on her arms. "It wasn't fear then, either. Kate...!"

She pulled away from him. "I...I've got to get to the airport," she said quickly.

He studied her in a silence tight

with emotion. "Come walk with me. One last time, Kate, and I'll let you go."

I'll let you go. Her eyes closed against the finality of those quiet words. But I don't want you to let me go! she thought miserably. If only I were older and more sophisticated and rich...

"All right," she agreed softly.

The lake was quiet. Not even a motorboat was stirring, and far away there was the silvery cry of seagulls against the horizon.

Inevitably, they came to Cambridge's land as they walked, to the log where Kate was sitting that long-ago day when he ran her off the beach. She dropped down on it and crossed her arms over her knees as she reached down to pluck a blade of grass to worry in her nervous fingers. She couldn't imagine why he wanted to talk to her, why he was behaving so strangely. He didn't seem to want to hurt her, now. But...why?

He stood at the lake's edge with a cigarette in his big hand, staring out across the choppy waters of the lake to the thick pine trees on the shore across the cove.

"It's been a long time since we found each other here," he remarked quietly.

"I was just thinking that," she remarked. Chill bumps were rising on her arms, because it was fall weather and the air off the lake was chilly.

"I threw you off my property," he recalled with a smile, "And you didn't even bother to argue with me. I took that for arrogance, little one, but it wasn't, was it? You aren't the argumentative type."

"I was afraid to argue with you," she admitted softly.

He turned. "Am I such an ogre, Kate?" he asked her. His eyes swept

over her hunched body. "You're
cold!"

"It's all right," she murmured.
"Just a chill."

He threw down the cigarette and sat
next to her on the log, folding her
against his big, warm body.

"Better?" he asked at her ear.

Better?! It was heaven, or as close
as she ever hoped to get on earth. Her
eyes closed and she savored the feel
and scent of him. Unconsciously, her
cheek nestled lovingly against his
broad chest.

"You're very warm," she murmured softly.

"You're soft," he mused. "Like a
warm feather pillow. You may look
thin, but you don't feel it."

She smiled in spite of herself.
"Skinny was how you put it."

His arms tightened. "Don't remind
me of what a fool I was," he muttered.
"I feel bad enough about it already."

"Why should you? I deserved it."

"No," he corrected. "No, Kate, you didn't. I should have known weeks ago. The signs were all there. But I was blind, in more ways than one."

"You didn't tell me on the phone that you could see again," she whispered.

"It was going to be a surprise," he told her. "I left Yama in New York, and I'd planned...well," he sighed, "never mind. It was a surprise, all right, but not the one I had in mind. I couldn't wait to see you—really see you. I dreamed of what it was going to be like when I walked in the door. And then I had to go blow hell out of my own dream with the first words I said to you." He sighed heavily. "Kate, if there was any way I could take it back...."

"It isn't wise to try and go backward," she said.

"I suppose not." He rocked her gently in his arms. "Why are you going away?"

"I...well, I don't work for you anymore, and..." she faltered.

"I thought you enjoyed living with me," he mused. "Part of the time, at least."

Her eyes closed. "I did," she admitted. "But it's over now. You'd never forget..."

His finger came down to cover her soft mouth and he looked down at her quietly. "Kate, I forget everything when I hold you," he said solemnly. "My God, honey, if you go now, I'll need a reason to get up in the mornings. I'll need a reason to breathe!"

She stared at him incredulously, not sure that she wasn't hearing things. "But you're a millionaire," she whispered. "I've got nothing...!"

"Neither have I, without you," he said shortly. His eyes burned over her face. "I have nothing unless I have you, is that clear enough? What the hell does money matter? Wouldn't you like to live in a cave with me, Kate? Wouldn't you live in a cave with me if I'd been a poor man?"

Tears trembled in her wide, soft eyes and started to overflow. She couldn't even manage an answer through the lump in her throat.

"When Maude told me about you this morning, I wanted to cut my throat," he said tightly. "Remembering what I'd said and done to you, and that look I couldn't understand in your eyes before you walked away from me—as if you could forgive me for killing you!—it hurt like hell...God, Kate!" he groaned, his eyes narrow with pain.

"It's all right," she said gently, sitting quietly in his arms, watching him intently, her heart bursting with the joy of loving him.

He searched her eyes for a long time with an unblinking curiosity that made ripples in her bloodstream.

"All that love I see in your eyes," he whispered huskily, "is it all for me, Kate?"

Her face went scarlet and she tried to hide her eyes from him, but he turned her face back.

"I'm years too old for you," he observed. "Bad tempered, spoiled for my own way. And you're just a baby. It might just be infatuation, Kate."

"Why don't you say what you mean?" she asked, lowering her eyes to his brown throat. "You don't want a little nobody like me who...."

"Don't you ever say that again!" he said harshly, catching her chin in a vicelike grip to force her face up to his blazing eyes. "You're not a nobody. You're my woman. You're the only thing in the world I give a damn about."

She gaped at him, feeling her jaw drop at the content of the statement, and the ferocity with which he said it.

"Don't look so dumbfounded," he growled. "My God, I wonder which of us was the more blind? Didn't it ever occur to you that I already had a secretary? You intrigued me from the first minute. I heard your voice and I had to have you. There was no book. I don't even have a publisher, I did it to keep you busy. And when you got tangled up with that damned reporter, I could have broken your neck for you. I took you to St. Martin for reasons that didn't have the first thing to do with work. But then I got to thinking about how young you were, and about the fact that I might be blind for life, and I got cold feet." He sighed, turning his gaze out toward the lake. "The fall was a blessing in disguise because it made an operation possible that restored my vision. I couldn't

wait to get back to you. They wanted
to keep me another three or four days
but I dismissed myself and came anyway." He looked down at her hungrily, and his eyes said it all. "I
needed to see you, to be near you, to
touch you. It's been hell being away
from you, milkmaid. I never meant to
let you get that close. God knows, I
fought it every step of the way, even
to inviting Anna down for a few days.
That backfired, too. She only made me
appreciate you more. I wondered
when I kicked her out why I'd ever
been taken in by her."

She stared up at him with her heart
shimmering in her eyes. Unbelievably,
he seemed to be telling her that he
loved her. A shudder of pure delight
ran the length of her soft body.

His eyes darkened suddenly as he
caught the intensity of feeling he read
in hers. "Don't look at me like that,"
he said huskily.

Her slender hands linked behind his head. "Don't look at you like what?" she asked, trembling with mingled excitement and fear. The hunger she read in his eyes was monstrous, and she wasn't confident about her ability to satisfy it.

His big hands went to her back, lifting her up against him gently. "You're asking for trouble, milkmaid," he whispered at her mouth.

Her fingers dug into the thick hair at the nape of his neck. "I don't know very much," she murmured against his broad, hard mouth. "You'll have to teach me."

A shudder passed through the hard hands at her back. "What a delicious thought," he laughed softly. "The darkness and you in my bed, loving me..."

"Garet!" she gasped.

His lips parted hers expertly, hungrily. "Tell me you love me."

"Oh, don't you know how much?" she whispered fiercely.

"Not yet," he murmured. "Show me."

"Like this?" she asked, rising in his arms to press her mouth long and hard against his.

"More like this, little innocent," he murmured wickedly, and proceeded to teach her how very intimate a kiss could be.

She blushed when he finally stopped long enough to catch his breath, but a new, soft light was in the eyes that worshipped him openly.

"I'm going to marry you, Kate," he said unsteadily. "No half measures for us."

"Garet, what if I don't fit into your world?" she asked seriously.

"We'll make one of our own," he replied simply. He brushed the wild hair away from her cheek with a tender hand. "I want a son with you," he said huskily. "I want a houseful of children."

Her eyes sketched his face. "Dark-haired little boys with green eyes...."

He crushed her mouth under his, roughly, hungrily, possessively. "Don't tempt me," he said tightly. "I want you like hell."

"I wouldn't stop you," she said softly. "Anything you want, Garet. Anything."

He smiled down at her. "I know that. I want you, for keeps. I could walk through fire to get to you." He pressed his lips to her forehead. "Let's go and tell Maude, before things get out of hand. I want you in white when you walk down that aisle to me, as old-fashioned as that may sound."

She smiled back. "Maude will be glad to know you didn't drown me in the lake."

"She knew better than that." He

laughed softly. "The first thing she
said to me this morning was that I had
a nasty way of treating the people who
love me most. When she made me understand who you really were, I
couldn't get to you fast enough.
You'll never know how I felt when I
walked into that room and you backed
away from me." His eyes searched
hers. "I wanted to go through the
damned floor. Kate, I didn't hurt you,
did I? Nothing was broken...?"

"You didn't push me," she said
gently. "I'm just bruised."

"Later, I'll kiss them all better," he
promised.

"Oh, you can't," she said without
thinking as her hands went to her
blouse.

"Oh, can't I?" he murmured with
a glint in his eyes. "God, I'm glad I
can see, now!"

She blushed to the roots of her hair
and ran ahead of him up the beach.

Far away, on the porch of her cabin, Maude Niccole watched the two of them running along the lake's edge. There were tears in her eyes as she went inside to put on the coffee.

*   *   *   *   *

Where love comes alive™

From first love to forever, these love stories are
for today's woman with traditional values.

Silhouette® Desire

A highly passionate, emotionally powerful
and always provocative read.

Silhouette®

SPECIAL EDITION™

Emotional, compelling stories that capture the
intensity of living, loving and creating a family in
today's world.

Silhouette

INTIMATE MOMENTS™

A roller-coaster read that delivers romantic thrills
in a world of suspense, adventure and more.

Visit Silhouette at www.eHarlequin.com

SDIR2

eHARLEQUIN.com

| community | membership |
| buy books | authors | online reads | magazine | learn to write |

magazine

♥——————————————— **quizzes**

Is he the one? What kind of lover are you? Visit the **Quizzes** area to find out!

♥——————————— **recipes for romance**

Get scrumptious meal ideas with our **Recipes for Romance.**

♥——————————————— **romantic movies**

Peek at the **Romantic Movies** area to find Top 10 Flicks about First Love, ten Supersexy Movies, and more.

♥——————————————— **royal romance**

Get the latest scoop on your favorite royals in **Royal Romance.**

♥——————————————————— **games**

Check out the **Games** pages to find a ton of interactive romantic fun!

♥——————————————— **romantic travel**

In need of a romantic rendezvous? Visit the **Romantic Travel** section for articles and guides.

♥——————————————————— **lovescopes**

Are you two compatible? Click your way to the **Lovescopes** area to find out now!

Silhouette® —

where love comes alive—online...

Visit us online at
www.eHarlequin.com

SINTMAG

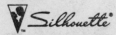